DIRK NECESSARY

A MAN'S MAN JOURNEY

KELLY S. WARD

ANTINOMY PUBLISHING

Book cover by Rebekah L. Potter

Illustrations by Rebekah L. Potter and Kelly S. Ward

First Edition 2025

ISBN 979-8-9930875-1-1

For information about special discounts available for bulk purchases, sales promotions, fund-raising and educational needs, contact Antinomy Publishing LLC at antinomypublishing@gmail.com.

Published by Antinomy Publishing LLC
P.O. Box 51
Williamsburg, New Mexico 87942

Dedicated to the following:

For the boys who will soon be men. Don't let them tell you that there is only one way to become a man. And, just as importantly, don't deny yourself the gift of becoming one. The bottom line, it's your responsibility. No shirking allowed. We need you to become the fullest expression of your authentic selves.

I tilled acres of emotional soil to be capable of writing. This was something I hadn't known I needed to do. The credit for my transformation and this book rests with one person. Potter.

1

SILENCING THE TEARS

A full school year had passed and I hadn't grown even an inch. Still dead last. Smallest. Weakest. A real loser's loser. A brutal verdict of my standing in the world.

On the bright side, the kids only remembered two names, the first and last on the list. History made by yours truly. Four years in a row. A name never forgotten. My legacy.

I hated it. My original name, the one I started life with. The one printed at the bottom of the list posted on the gym wall. My stomach in a constant ache from the knowledge that it could be written or spoken at any moment for all to hear or see. I hid from bullies and even teachers but my name was impossible to avoid. And, there it was staring back at me.

I stood in front of the list, stomach acid boiling over, and contemplated a worse situation. A disciplined habit.

Each school year started and ended with the 'Measure Up' in gym class. Mandated by the President of the United State of America, this invasive physical assessment included, body height and weight, push-up, sit-up, and pull-up counts, 100-yard sprint and one-mile run times. The results were posted, publicly, for god and everyone to see. To scrutinize. Someone had to be first. Someone had to be last. Logical. A simple truth. I knew the first position was not mine to hope for. Not to be last, that was a reasonable wish.

If only I had a bottle from which to rub a wish-granting genie.

"Maybe next year, eh?" Jimmy Pockets said as he scanned the list. That wasn't his real name. The Jimmy part was but the kids mostly called him Pockets on account of how his hands were in his pockets most of the day. Pants pockets. Jacket pockets. Shirt pockets. His mom had even sewn pockets on clothes that didn't have pockets to begin with. Including the t-shirts he wore in gym class. Pockets had just found his name listed right above mine. Second from the last.

Two more sit-ups than me. Like being a nickel short for an ice cream cone. Had I known, I could have found a nickel somewhere just as I could have found three sit-ups.

No time to muse about the would of, could of, should of's. It was clear Pockets needed a cheerful confidence boost, after all, he was pretty low down on the list.

My mother had a saying. She got it from her father who got it from his father and on and on through the generations. Kind of a family motto. A bad day can always get worse. Her comforting words for every challenge of a young boy's life. Teased at school? Skinned knee? Poor test score? All made better knowing it could get worse.

No surprise that these were her last words to me. The letter came in the mail. She had been gone for a few days. Not unusual. Except that this time she hadn't returned. An envelope delivered by the postman. Her handwriting, addressed to me, a short good-bye.

Hey Kid,

Keep up with your studies. Try a little harder to make friends, can't be a loner all your life. And, don't worry, you will grow soon, I know it. And when you do, you will be a strong and capable young man. I needed to leave. Sorry that I didn't have time to say goodbye. I hope someday you will be able to understand. Don't worry about me. Remember, a bad day can always get worse.

Mom

Just like that, no more brewed coffee and French toast aromas to wake to. No more John Denver or Neil Diamond belted out from the turntable. No more mom. Only memories. That was sixteen months, twenty-two days ago.

Every stormy day has a darker cloud on the horizon. Pockets should hear it from me first. "A small bump in the road. No point in dwelling on the past. Mother says, a bad day can always get worse," I said.

Pockets considered this familial wisdom. "Yeah...I guess so. What are you going to do this summer?" A change of subject to avoid an emotional moment. I played along. No point in picking at an open wound.

Summer vacation was starting in four short hours. Just had to get through lunch and a final desk and locker inspection. "Dr. Schroeder says I should hit a growth spurt soon so I am keeping my plans to a minimum. Might need to just sit around and grow."

"Well, see you next year, Kid."

The final bell rang right on time. I sprinted home from school. Three miles in the desert's afternoon sun. Like an oasis, the house emerged in the distance. No lofty promise of sanctuary but it was my shelter.

I locked the door handle, chain lock, the bolt latch, and two deadbolts. "Safety first." Dad always said. The whole commotion and its mechanistic signature pin-balled through the tight entryway, passed the washer and dryer, ricocheted off the bifold door, and echoed back to me. The house's daily reminder that I was protected from the outside world like a coal miner in a collapsed shaft.

I pulled the bifold door and slipped into the kitchen. The smell of my father's aftershave lingered. I must have just missed him. I ignored the note on the counter. My ears filled with organ music from a Dracula film. Looming danger.

I crumpled the note, squeezed it hard in my fist, and ran to my bedroom.

Hey Kid,

I waited for you as long as I could. I found work. Out of state. Only job I could get. Have to be there in the morning. Groceries in the fridge. I'll send money. Should be home by the end of the summer. Mr. Carter will bring feed. Keep Balthazar alive.

Pops

Father wouldn't be back. The family motto sung out. The house went from quiet to empty.

"Keep Balthazar alive." I read aloud.

Marcus Aurelius said, "Death smiles at all of us, but all a man can do is smile back." Which was why when the tears streamed from my cheek onto the wrinkled note, I smiled and laughed. A defiant bellow.

A man can do no more.

AT THE FORK IN THE ROAD

The pitchfork effortlessly released the hay into Balthazar's feed bin. I had read him my father's note and told him the results of the 'Measure Up". He considered our situation. I knew he would eat before he spoke. He didn't like to talk on a hungry stomach. I added two scoops of oats to the bin and busied myself with his water trough.

He lifted his snout from his meal. "Kid," I peeked out from his stall. Everyone called me Kid on account of me despising my real name. My protest started five years ago. I simply refused to acknowledge anyone who called me by my given name. Young Goat, Kid, was my compromise. Its usefulness was beginning to wear with age. Balthazar continued, "you are boxed in. Only one question to ask and answer, are you a man or a mouse?"

That hit heavy. I felt the weight of the universe and its gods demand an answer. No escape from their soul crippling stare. My answer should have been definitive. Automatic. My parts were all male. Though the thought of scurrying through life along the floorboards didn't sound so horrible. My stomach turned. I smiled and laughed. Never giving the tears a chance to build.

"I am a man, Balthazar. A strong, capable, man's man. It may not look like it to anyone else, but I will be a great man. Not sure what that means, but that's me." Take that universe.

"To be great, Kid, you have to know the greats."

Balthazar's pep talk sent me to the library each week. A summer filled reading about the great emperors, generals, thinkers, and tinkerers. Healing salve of knowledge and inspiration to dispel the despair. Nearly three months older and all the more wiser, as the new school year approached.

Snack time. An afternoon ritual. Sustenance of the body: saltines, cheddar cheese, and strawberry jelly. Eaten sandwich style. Sustenance of the mind: Napoleon Bonaparte, Napoleon I, Emperor to the French, King of Italy, and Protector of the Confederation of the Rhine.

Laid open before me, *The Napoleonic era, a pictorial history of the man and the empire he built.* Page 155, a portrait, *Emperor Napoleon in his study at the Tuileries.* Opposite this, page 156, a portrait, *Bonaparte crossing the Alps.* Both by Jacques-Louis David. Both were classic Napoleon. The first, standing dressed in his white culottes de Casimir tucked into his low-cut boots, right hand half shoved into his vest coat just above the navel. The second, valiantly atop his trusted steed, tight white breeches tucked into black knee-high riding boots, a madder cape in full flutter, horse reared back and prepared to charge forth. Page after page, more times than not, Napoleon appeared in white pants. That felt significant. A sign I was destined to heed. And, heed, I did indeed.

Earlier that day, I carded myself to Bleeker's, the only clothing store in town. The coming school year, ninth grade, my first of high school, was scheduled to start the next day. I aimed for a breakout year. Bleeker's would help make it happen. Timeless Fashions for a Modern World was their tagline. Mr. and Mrs. Bleeker founded the store in 1800 and something. They still sat behind the register everyday. The youthful employees tended to the customers and the cash register. The two of them spent their days commenting on the customer's purchases. I enjoyed listening to them. It was a history lesson with each comment.

"Teddy Roosevelt wore just that same kerchief when he charged the ramparts at San Juan. Kept the sun off his neck and the sweat off his uniform."

"James Marshall had cinched his pants with that very belt the day he struck it rich at Sutter's Mill. He and that belt launched the California Gold Rush. His lucky belt, he called it. It held his pants 'till the day he died."

"Amelia Earhart, flew solo across the Atlantic in 1932 in that blouse. Fourteen hours and fifty-six minutes in the cockpit. The Queen greeted her on her arrival. Look at the photo, not a single wrinkle on Amelia's shirt."

Every Monday afternoon through the summer, the postman delivered an envelope. $44.00. Cash. *Grocery Money* my father's handwritten note read. Same words. Same amount. Each week. I kept every note in an old pickle jar fashioned up like a piggy bank. What I didn't spend on food, I saved in a shoe box kept on a closet shelf. A slush fund for school clothes and supplies.

My squirreled away stash set me up, in the fashion sense, for a winning school year. I went for several classics, Nike Pegasus sneakers and Levi 501 jeans, then gambled on a few trendy items, a wide-collared polyester paisley button down and a black belt with silver rhinestones. My prized purchase was a pair of white jeans.

"You know kid, Napoleon wore those same pants on his journey to battle the Austrians in Italy," Mr. Bleeker said.

A knowing smile rose on my lips. "Exactly, Mr. Bleeker. This is my year of conquest. Figured they worked for Napoleon, they will work for me," I replied.

At the kitchen table, saltines and Napoleon. I considered the

Emperor, gallant and commanding as he straddled his powerful horse. His white britches gleaming in the sun. I considered my white jeans and Balthazar. I smiled.

In an instant, a burst of enthusiasm enlivened me. Visions of me galloping onto the school house steps like Napoleon crossing the Alps. It was all possible. I had the pants. I had the horse. Yes, yes, yes. I had the horse. Balthazar, my trusted steed. Two peas in a pod. Never a better friend than he. We would lay our lives down for one another. I ran to my room to put on the pants, paisley shirt, belt, and shoes. Smashing. Balthazar was the lynchpin. I needed him to be impressed.

Having a horse was not synonymous with riding a horse or having a ridable horse. Those notions, having and riding, collided only on Balthazar's schedule. Said schedule was never published by the brute, Balthazar. I understood that at its core, his mood was the ultimate determiner and he was impervious to coercion. No amount of oats, apples, sugar cubes, bathing, or brushing, influenced him. How Balthazar determined his availability to be a horse, in the ridable sense of a horse, remains one of my life's greatest mysteries. The whole affair was mood dependent. Every day was a new day in his world.

Time to figure out if Balthazar would play a prominent role in my conquest of high school. To be fair of Balthazar's situation, it was two o'clock P.M. He was accustomed to eating at about six A.M. most days. He was both excited to see me and suspicious that I seemed refreshed and enthusiastic. I had a pep in my step. The stylish outfit and Napoleon's book were his clues that something was afoot.

I could see him struggle with a decision about his participation in my scheme. His hesitation, I thought, was premature as we had not even discussed the plan. In hindsight, my singing to him probably tipped him off to what he expected to be an unreasonable request. His defiant spirit weakened as I added additional oats to his hay. He dug into his breakfast as if he hadn't eaten for days. I sang another song while I brushed his coat.

Clearly, I had come at a good time for Balthazar, so I hit him with the plan. "I will ride you, like Napoleon at Marengo, to the school steps in a triumphant conquest. Nobility arrived. Honor and adornment awaits at the end of a short three mile walk. Me upon my trusted steed." He lifted his snout to get a good look at me, you know, eye-to-eye, man-to-man stuff. Had he confirmed the boldness of the plan or estimated my sanity? Hard to tell from day-to-day what that look meant.

I opted for the first interpretation and repeated the plan, emphasized his role in it, and reinforced that the day would be strenuous so rest was advisable. "Glory is assured." I said.

The plan was falling perfectly into place.

My thoughts shifted to a triumphant march upon the school.

Balthazar was not the kind of horse you should turn your back to. There ought to be an idiom of sorts about such things. Maybe, converte te ad equum; accipit te momordit. Turn your back to a horse; expect to be bit. Latin always made situations sound grand. Balthazar taught me that. He often spoke in Latin. "A byproduct of my heritage, I am afraid," he would say. He was Lusitano by breed. Though not pure blood.

It turned out that Balthazar had reconsidered the plan while I cleaned the stalls. He had tip-hoofed behind me as I went for the gate. No sooner had I reached out for the latch then my shoulder erupted in pain as Balthazar chomped down on skin, muscle, what little there was, and bone.

Balthazar had spoken.

I went to the garage. My bicycle tires filled with air. Plan B - Alternate Transportation - was secured.

The morning pedal to school, uneventful. The locker lined hallway, the conqueror conquered.

There are only two occasions on which someone's derriere should heat up. Not the cozy warmth under the blanket heat. The searing, "I think my buttocks are 'o fire" type of heat. Around the campfire on a cold night and testing flatulence flammability. I was engaged in neither. Hence my delayed response.

I stood boldly at my locker when my locker neighbor arrived. "My name is Tina," she said. "Martina, if Tina is too hard."

My first high school conversation. If this is high school, I am glad I showed up. I thought.

"Martina does have a soft melodic ring to it. I agree. Tina is too hard. Feels demanding when I say Tina." I leaned hard on the T and lengthened the A. "T-n-AA."

She giggled. Not a high pitched or nervous giggle. A sincere expression of jocularity. "You're funny," she said.

The new school year was off to a wonderful start. The white pants worked miracles.

We were interrupted by an emerging situation. Martina alerted me to the smoke. During our short exchange of pleasantries, someone used their lighter to burn the backside of my pants in the most inappropriate location. It was like the time I cut the tip of my thumb off. I was julienne-ing carrots, moving fast, julienned the tip right off before my brain had a chance to register the pain. My brain was focused on Martina and didn't register that my butt was on fire until she said, "I think your butt is on fire."

SUBCONSCIOUSLY LOOKING FOR A FIGHT

That Martina knew a thing or two. My butt was on fire. Spontaneous combustion ruled out.

Disbelief became anger. I turned to face my tormentor. Fester, Stevie Fester. He stood, lighter in hand, a smug smile. He wasn't alone. He took three easy steps backward. His friends stepped forward. Protection. Intimidation. Overwhelming numbers.

I was left to hang my head in resignation to my own weakness and cowardice.

Turned out this would be another school year just like all the previous, I thought. No point in sticking around.

I pushed the bicycle. Not in the mood to ride. A slow walk into the desert morning.

A half mile from home, the neighbor, Mr. Adler, had piled boxes at the end of the drive. Some taped neatly. Some left open, their contents partly out of the boxes. "Whatcha' doing, Mr. Adler?" I asked.

"Time to clear out Fin's room, I suppose."

Fin died the previous year. It was a big deal for the town.

Star athlete. Played every sport. He worked at the sawmill. An accident with logs or some such. Everyone in town was at the funeral.

Hard to know what to say. I fumbled through one of the boxes, mostly to keep from the awkward silence. "I am sorry about Fin, Mr. Adler."

"Each day is a little easier. If there is something you want, you are welcomed to it. The things that mean something to Mrs. Adler and me, I put away. This is mostly stuff he had on his walls and trinkets laying around his room. They're headed to the trash."

There were several posters neatly rolled and bundled protruding from the top of the stack. I investigated.

Walter Payton, the great running back for the Chicago Bears, leapt head first over the tangled mob of the Bears' and Packers' front lines. Not a football fan but his was one of the names the jocks would talk about on Monday mornings. Reggie Jackson, baseball's right fielder in his New York Yankees' uniform, his bat swung out wide in front of him, another home run. Baseball wasn't my thing. The rock band, KISS, demonic Gene Simmons' tongue out. The Starchild, Paul Stanley, a lady killer. Perfect for the inside of my bedroom door. I unrolled the last poster. "Wow!" I said. Mr. Adler walked up with another box in his arms. "Who is Heather, Mr. Adler?"

"Oh yeah. That was Fin's favorite. Heather Locklear. She is on television, TJ Hooker. You haven't watched it?"

"I like TV but I guess I haven't seen that one. I only get a couple of channels. Antenna is so so."

"Well, I think Fin sure enjoyed those posters. I would hear him in there. Talking away. Guess he was figuring life out loud with athletes, rock stars, and an actress. I thought it odd." Mr. Adler gazed off toward the sky. I followed his eyes. Didn't see anything except blue sky and a wispy cloud. He turned back to me. "...but, he would go into his room agitated, like young men get, and reemerge hours later, calm and ready to talk to Mrs. Adler and me."

"Would it be alright if I take these two?"

"Not much into sports, eh?"

"No sir. But the night is still young." I chuckled. Heard that phrase in a movie. I liked how it sounded.

Mr. Adler studied me. "First day of school, isn't it?" I nodded. "The day is still young. Why aren't you at the school?" It was his turn to chuckle.

"Left early. Tired of being pushed around. Looks like it will be another year at the short end of the stick."

"I think I understand. Your father still working out of town?" I nodded. "If you need anything, come on back. Mrs. Adler and I are always home. You better take all four posters. Best not to break up the set. They seemed to be helpful to Fin, I bet they will help you also."

"Thanks Mr. Adler."

"You know, Kid, we all faced the moment life asked us to choose to be a man or be a mouse? You might be face-to-face with your moment."

Mr. Adler's words looped in my head. A tornado siren warning of imminent danger. I knew he spoke the truth. I felt it. Every boy must. The end of the dependence, the innocence. It should be a moment of joy and anticipation. Leaving the protective shelter for an adventurous world. Fear reigned supreme for me. Fear of the hazards of confrontation and competition. Fear of failure and embarrassment. Fear of the unknown. The half mile walk home lasted a lifetime as I played out every conceivable catastrophe that lay ahead. Unhelpful.

I remembered Hippocrates' advice, starve a fever, feed a

sadness. A snack would cheer my mood and bring focus to my swirling mind. The situation demanded something special. Toast, butter thick as frosting, cinnamon and sugar dusting the top as if blown in on a sirocco. By the third toast I felt better. Ready to face my realities.

I had a whole day and nothing to do. My early release from school was beginning to look fortuitous. A normally busy schedule unexpectedly opened. Finally, time enough to tidy my room and none-too-soon. I was down to my last clean pair of undershorts.

Ten minutes later, clothes were in the washer and the surfaces wiped. Room clean. Plenty of daylight left. The rolled posters on the kitchen counter caught my eye as I emerged from the hallway. Perfect timing. The room was ready for visitors and I was in the mood for decorating.

KISS was easy, Gene, Paul, Ace, and Eric stood guard behind the bedroom door. The four boogeymen waiting to spring on an unsuspecting intruder. "Okay, gents. We are going to Rock And Roll All Nite. Anyone steps into the room uninvited, You Shout It Out Loud," I chuckled.

Reggie Jackson swung for the fences next to the bathroom entrance. "Well, Mr. October, looks like you will be in the clean up position. Let's get 'em round the bases." This was getting kind of fun.

Walter Payton leapt for victory high above the dresser. "You look good, Sweetness. This is a big year. I need for some of your grace and strength to rub off on me."

Heather Locklear smiled and winked at me from her prominent position directly across from my bed. My first sight as I woke in the morning and my last as I lay down at night. "Hello, Ms. Locklear. Sorry that I didn't know you existed until today but maybe I'll be your leading man one day."

I was pleased with how my room looked. It felt as if the posters were supposed to be there. They fit. Hand to glove.

"Alright, you all just hang in here. I'll be back after dinner."

The rest of the day was shooting baskets, fourteen out of one hundred sixty-four attempts. Solid numbers. I had a craving for barbecue that evening. Fried bologna sandwich with BBQ sauce and mayonnaise. Dessert, half carton of butterscotch ripple ice cream and chocolate sauce.

Sublime.

Maybe it was the unfamiliar environment, clean room and new faces. Or maybe it was the ice cream before bed that caused the unsettled sleep and vivid dream.

A beast of unfathomable horror chased me through the dream version of my hometown. As he neared overtaking me, I turned and battled, hand-to-hand, limb-to-limb, fighting off the beast. Each time I would sprint ahead, it would catch me and the wrestling match would ensue once more. Over and over, this happened. In its clutches, entangled, and tumbling together, temple-to-temple, we spoke without speaking. "Ego sum Magnus Mendacium," he said. "I am the Big Lie. The lie people tell themselves that sabotages their success, joy, and love for self and others."

Mendacium told me he hunts at night when the tricksters of Doubt and Loathing are opening the unconscious minds of the sleeping masses. He hunts, he continued, for those who do not protect themselves, who mask their fears in a conscious air of overconfidence and superiority, but for whom their subconscious has left open the gate to their true selves. I froze at the realization of the truth of the big lie that was this beast.

In my moment of hesitation, he escaped my clutches and disappeared down the darkened street. I ran after Mendacium in a frantic search. Nowhere. He was gone. I stood dead center of the road with only the sounds of my panting breath. And in the quiet that emerged, the moaning sounds of defeat and anxiety rose from the houses. I knew the beast had found his prey. Unable to protect the town's people. Inadequate. Weak. Hesitant. I woke in fright's cold sweat.

The room was deathly quiet.

"Bad dream?" A female voice called from the darkness.

4

NEW FRIENDS FROM STRANGE PLACES

"He had a bad dream," A male voice.

Still in dreamland, I thought. Dreams of waking. Dreams of voices. Smushed against the wall and the headboard, I cornered myself and held my breath through the darkness. Nothing there.

I stumbled to the bathroom. Splashed cold water on my face. Not awake. More cold water and a promise to keep the ice cream to two scoops, max. Is this lactose intolerance? I wondered.

"Feel better?" The female voice said I as reentered.

I flipped the light switch. I was alone.

"Hey there. Nightmare?" Her voice again.

I walked to the Heather Locklear poster. She winked. Speechless.

"Crazy, Crazy Night. Dreaming between the darkness and the light?" A male voice sang. I turned to see KISS' Gene Simmons staring at me.

I felt ill.

The walls began to close in. My vision turned kaleidoscopic with each poster in sharp relief to the wall. Likewise the faces of the posters in 3-D relief to their backgrounds. No ice cream before bed, ever again, I thought.

"Stop spinning, young man, you are making me dizzy." A new voice, Reggie Jackson.

"How...how are you all talking?" I stammered.

"You started it. And, thank you for the new home. My hair had no chance of surviving the grime and dust of the trash heap," Heather said.

"So, let's hear it, kid. What was the dream about," Walter said.

I figured I was still in the dream world, cold water and all. If I could dream about a monster, I could dream about talking posters. Nothing to lose, I recanted the dream.

"Man up. You've got to hit them like a freight train coming," Gene sang.

"I guess I am not that type of man. Fin probably was but not me," I said.

"Well, it is time you became one," Walter said. Silence. Walter continued, "You said this is a big year for you. Let's get to it."

"Can't just rush in willy nilly. A race is won at the starting line. Best to be considerate of where and when to start," I said. Regaining confidence. Anything can happen in the dream world.

"You start where you are. Start by starting. What man things are you already doing?"

"Doing? I dunno. I figured that I had man parts so I am a man, right?"

"We have another Fin situation on our hands, fellows," Heather said.

"It's not enough to be a man in that sense. You have to be seen being a man. You have to perform manly feats in front of other men," Reggie said.

"Do the things he says to do. He's worth a deuce. Tell him, Heather," Gene sang.

Worth a deuce? Confused. I turned to Heather. "Tell me what?"

"The business of show business is telling the world what it is to be a man and what it is to be a woman. First off, you have to look like a man. You need a mustache. You need to be tall. You need muscles. And you need a cigarette hanging from your lips."

"Best path to acting like a man is to play sports. Isn't that right, Walter?" Reggie said.

"Right. You also need to display your courage and bravery through the pursuit of danger. A man never backs down from a fight. You never let a Magnus Mendacium win."

"Don't forget about being a ladies' man," KISS' Starchild, Paul Stanley, said.

"And, you can't be afraid to get dirty. Step Up. No one leaves until the night is done. Makeup running and unshaven," Gene sang.

"Makeup could be interesting," I whispered, hand to chin. No whiskers. Off to a slow start, I thought reaching for the light switch. That was a strange dream. The last words of the night. Thankfully, my own.

Morning came around too soon. Awake but afraid to open my eyes. The posters. Unsure of which was more unsettling their speaking or their man-making list.

School wouldn't wait. I sprang out of bed and into the bathroom. The urge to look at the posters resisted. Cleaned up and in need of clothes. Cautious. Maybe the posters were still asleep. Silly. It was just a dream. Courage. I walked directly to the dresser, found a T-shirt, socks, and jeans. Wrestled into them as I crossed toward the door. I glanced back to the room. No movement. No voices. Relief.

The previous day's early exit from school hadn't raised

alarms so the reintegration into the school routine was seamless. I stuck to the baseboards, nooks, and crannies to avoid the bullies and most of the other students. I ate lunch in a far corner of the cafeteria so as not to disturb the others.

The week settled into a routine. Woke early to greet Heather and the fellows. Thankfully, no return greetings. Fed Balthazar and off to school.

Each afternoon, I tossed my bag and myself on the bed and said, "Well, another day in the history books." I spoke to each poster as if I reported on the day's events. Social interactions and gossip to Heather. Girls to KISS. Gym class to Reggie. Educational highlights to Walter. Fantastical stories of my day.

Friday, a long first week was over. The freedom of the weekend. I threw my book bag on the bed. "It's the weekend everyone. What shall we do?" I said to the room.

"We thought about your dream," Heather said.

Oh boy. Not again, I thought.

"Time to turn your imagined world into reality," Walter said.

"I want to know, does a frozen river flow? Because there is a fine line between the truth and how we want it to be," Gene sang.

Good question. Does a frozen river flow? Lost in thought.

"The town needs a herald. A town crier. Their Paul Revere to wake them to the truth and the lie," Reggie said.

I hadn't eaten ice cream all week. The constant ingestion of knowledge, four days full, had me disoriented. A possibility. Short circuit of the brain. Might need to take a few days off of school, I said to myself.

"You must warn them of the beast of unfathomable horror, of Magnus Mendacium," Heather said.

"Opportunities to be brave and courageous, to be a man, don't appear often," Walter said.

Silence. Time to think. The sudden onset of voices in my

head should have sent me to seek a doctor's care. Thing was, the voices weren't in my head. I knew those kinds of voices. These were real. Like with Balthazar, if you knew the language, you heard the words.

One man's subliminal, was another's screaming mob.

I cast aside worry and focused on the wisdom of my new friends' suggestion. I drifted off to sleep. Magnus Mendacium met me in dreamland. "The town will be asleep soon and I will be waiting," he said.

Where was Paul Revere when you needed him? "I will warn them," I said.

Magnus laughed, "I will beat you to their doorstep. You will be too late."

Naps were better than overnight sleep for mind work. Solutions generated by the subconscious were more readily available after a nap.

"I got it!" I said to the room. All eyes were on me. "The Quick Draw Special."

Dad's Colt .45, single action revolver. Samuel Colt, himself, coined it, The Quick Draw Special. My father practiced his own version of a quick draw while watching old western movies late at night. I held the chrome smoke wagon once. Briefly. Dad warned me never to play with it. I was just a kid then and I kept away. Certainly, embarking on a man quest was reason enough to grant permission. With dad out of town, the decision fell on me. For the sake of the town's people, I relented. The embargo was lifted.

"I will be the herald. The Paul Revere. I will ride atop Balthazar to the town square, fire the Colt .45, the sleeping masses will wake, and I will warn them of the impending danger," I stated.

"Flawless," Heather said.

"Yes, a revolver, expertly handled, imputes authority. They will surely heed your warnings," Reggie said.

A mission of such importance would certainly compel Balthazar to participate. In fact, his enthusiasm to charge headlong into danger was the worry. I wondered if I could ride him at those speeds. His determination overtaking my command of the reins. The risks of hero work. Balthazar loved spontaneity, better to brief him on the plan after dinner.

Speaking of which. An occasion of this magnitude required a special meal at a special place. And, I had a craving. Dick's Cafe. The locals called it Dirty Dick's. Their chocolate chip pancakes with raspberry syrup were sublime. I couldn't help but wonder, as I drained the syrup jar on my stack of yummy, which of my fellow diners would have fallen victim to the Beast's lie tonight.

Would Magnus Mendacium get the father who sat oblivious to the conversation of his wife and three teenaged children? Or, the middle-aged man who made the short walk from his red sports car to the entrance and now scanned the room for approving glances? Or, the young woman who held an air of dismissiveness for all the diner to see? Which of these masks would I shatter tonight? Or which would provide the pathway to their soul for Magnus Mendacium?

Full belly. Full courage. Time to spring the plan on Balthazar and watch his excitement mount.

"The town needs us Balthazar. We are their only hope."

"Engua para d' ata. Give a pledge and trouble is at hand," Balthazar snorted.

Riddles.

Balthazar had a habit of speaking in riddles. This one meant he declined. He was resolute. Balthazar's reluctance made Heather sad but I knew my reliable hand-me-down ten speed would serve a suitable replacement. Though not elaborate, the plan was foolproof.

I would pedal to the exact center of Main Street, stand in the middle of the road, fire several rounds from the Colt .45 revolver, and wait for the townsfolk to emerge from their homes.

I expected they would recognize that I came with a message of hope and salvation. Assured of my benevolent intent, they would gather around me to receive the secret that only I possessed.

The street was quiet. Quiet even by our town's standard.

"Perfect!" I proclaimed to nobody.

Balthazar would surely regret his shortsighted decision making.

I took a moment to review my speech notes and to fully commit to my course of action. The magnitude of which matched my preparedness as I had developed a passion for movies. Westerns on Saturday afternoons and gangster shoot 'em ups on Saturday nights. Also, I was quite proficient with the various weapons of the arcade shooting games having spent several days over the summer at the arcade. Shooting was kind of my thing. The fact I hadn't actually fired a gun before that night never entered my mind. I was ready.

I reached my right hand into my backpack. Took a firm grip on the .45 Quick Draw Special. Having loaded the weapon in the safety of my home, there was nothing more to do than raise it high above my head, pull back on the hammer, and squeeze the trigger.

Kapow!

5

FAINTED SPELLS AND MUSTACHED DREAMS

S amuel Colt sure knew how to build revolvers. It was almost as if the Quick Draw Special didn't need me. The trigger was remarkably smooth. The hammer released with the slightest of effort. I hadn't felt my finger squeeze the trigger.

Three sensations instantly overwhelmed me. First, the flash of ignited gunpowder expelling out the end of the barrel blinded me. Second, the audible report of the violent explosion had the simultaneous impact on my eardrums as to render me deaf and start a ringing that lasted for several weeks. Third, I learned about recoil. It would be several years before I knew that specific word. In that instant of squeezing the trigger, however, my arm thrust behind my head with a force that made me speculate if my arm was still attached. Recoil.

The smoke cleared. Assessment.

The revolver was still in my hand.

I could see.

My arm, though sore, moved as normal.

Eardrum ringing numbness, if that was a thing. Deaf. Not a

problem. I did not expect to listen to any of the town's folk. I was there to proclaim. That I could still do.

I surveyed the street. No lights flicked on. No curtains fluttered with the peering of the curious. I had five shots left. Undaunted. A valuable lesson learned. I raised the .45 revolver above my head with both hands. I kept my eyes averted and focused ahead of me for the second shot. The ears were already ringing. What further damage could another round possibly inflict?

Reflecting on my personal experience, I am of the opinion that a fifteen-year-old should not shoot the Colt .45 Quick Draw Special.

The blast report of the second shot rendered my ears useless until nearly noon the following day. The decision to look away from the gun barrel allowed me to ride home safely despite the blood. The two-handed grip on the revolver served to guide the recoiling gun directly into my forehead. The hammer functioned as a merciless blade. The four-inch valley it carved into my scalp poured forth, what I estimated was a full pint of blood.

Even if people had emerged from their homes, I was rendered ineffective as a messenger. The town would have to fend off the Magnus Mendacium on their own.

The heavy silence of my bedroom told me all I needed to know. Reggie and Walter couldn't even look at me. I sensed they wanted off the wall. Successful people don't like to be around failures.

Several weeks passed before we could see the greater lessons. Or, speak to one another.

My ears had not healed. My forehead had. Sort of.

In the mirror, looking back at me, was the legacy of the Paul Revere and Magnus Mendacium incident. Grotesquely displayed at my hairline was a mishmash of angled and frayed tissue struggling to find a matching edge across the chasm created by the Colt .45 hammer. I felt the lingering pain of an underwhelmed performance.

"Scars make the man," Heather yelled from the bedroom.

Progress!

Her voice of hope lifted me from the belly of despair. No more subconscious at the helm. Dreams were for the dreamers. I was a man of action. The Captain of my own ship. Time to get organized.

"Okay, everyone," I called the meeting to order. "Let's review the list. Get mustache. Get tall. Get muscles. Smoke cigarettes. Be an athlete. Be brave and courageous. Be a ladies' man. And, get dirty. Is that it?"

"Got to fight, kid. Two-fisted to the end. No lies, no more alibis," Gene sang.

I wrote the list on the bathroom mirror. In red lipstick. Not just any red, Le Rouge St. Germaine. The name mattered. I have no idea why but it stuck with me.

The list reminded me, each morning and night, I was on a man-making mission and was leaving nothing to chance.

First up, Get Mustache. Enthusiasm jumpstarted.

The easiest to do and the most immediate in its impact. I mean, you see a mustache and your first thought is man. 100% man, manly, burly, virile, strong, and capable. A man's man. All the men had one, Magnum P.I. Every character in any western movie. Walker Texas Ranger had a mustache. Smoky and the Bandit had mustaches. Gomez Adams had a mustache. Isaac Washington from The Love Boat. He had a mustache. Yosemite Sam had a great mustache. Even the guy who used to tell us which movies were good, Gene Shalit, he had a mustache. Life imitating art.

The Horseshoe   The Pencil   The Walrus   The Handlebar

The Toothbrush

The Beardstache

The Pyramid

The Chevron and Goatee

Point is, at a glance, a mustache tells you a man is approaching. My first stop, the school library. With a practiced confidence, I approached the librarian, Mrs. McDermott. "I'll need all your books on mustache growing," I said.

Her disappointment sat between us like moist, stale air.

"Why would you want such a thing?" She said. "Mr. McDermott had a mustache when he returned from the war. It was the most disgusting thing I ever saw on him. I made him shave it immediately. He's never grown one since and we have been happily married for 37 years next Saturday. Besides, you're a child and by the looks of you, you probably won't be able to grow one for a very long time, if ever."

Mr. McDermott returned from the war with a mustache. He obviously survived untold battles and escaped the clutches of the enemy solely because he and his fellow band of brothers grew mustaches.

When men are around other men, unchecked by women, their mustaches are a gift to their fellow men.

Mrs. McDermott had proven my point and steeled my determination. But it was clear she could not be trusted. I was on my own. I found a book on makeup and costumes in the movie industry. Perfect.

Hollywood mustaches looked authentic. The magic of the movies. I found myself suddenly considering the unthinkable regarding Magnum P.I. No time for that. I shook off the thoughts and immersed myself in the craft of fake facial hair. It was a simple two ingredient process, real glue and fake hair. I had neither. Minor complication for which Mrs. McDermott, unwittingly, provided a solution.

As I approached the counter with the makeup book, I couldn't help but notice that Mrs. McDermott's face had shifted to the right by two inches. I don't mean she cocked her head to the right. I mean, her face had shifted under her head such that her bangs lay at her left temple. Reading had always made me dizzy, so I wasn't immediately concerned for her. She turned fully toward me, which amplified the distortion.

She must have felt how out of sorts she looked. "Oh my, this damn wig," she said. She took a firm grip on her hair and gave it a sharp tug to the left. That did the trick.

Odd what people get up to when they don't think others are watching.

Her words sparked a thought.

I didn't have a fake mustache like the people in the Hollywood book, so my initial plan was to ask Balthazar if I could cut a swatch off his mane. Inspired by the moment, a vision of me three years prior flashed into my mind.

Christmas Day had loomed on the horizon. I had mounted a search for hidden Christmas presents. The most forbidden room in the house, the parent's bedroom, offered the most promising location. I hadn't been there in years. Fortunately, mom and dad had preserved it exactly as I remembered. A quick peek under the bed. Nothing. Too easy. I moved to the closet.

Immediately upon opening the closet doors, I was face-to-face with two severed and faceless heads. My mother is a monster, I thought. I screamed like a little schoolgirl. I'm not sure why we slander girls by genderizing fear. I know genderizing is not a word, but it should be. The autonomic response to the fright I felt at the sight of the lifeless people living in my mother's closet was an age appropriate shriek. I recovered in the comfort of my room. The realization that the closet doors were still open forced my return.

Somewhere between the heart palpitations and the consideration of a call to the authorities, my curiosity took over. One of the heads wore a platinum shag hairstyle. The other, a reddish bob. I mustered the courage to snag the faceless head with the platinum shag off the shelf. Upon close examination no crimes had been committed.

No more than foam in the shape of a head wrapped in fabric. I named him Ichabod in honor of the initial impression he cast.

Though not as realistic as a puppet, he could talk none-the-less. With a bit of prodding he was quite expressive. He said he lost his body in a terrifying barbershop accident. The details were disturbing and not to be repeated in polite company. His big revelation, however, was that the shag was not permanently attached. My fingers ran through his course hair. I found it strange that, despite my efforts to mess up his hairdo, it would return to lay perfectly coifed. Evidently, his last barber was quite talented. He invited me to put it on. To wear someone else's hair, particularly one whose last haircut ended so dramatically, was unsettling. He chided encouragingly.

My first introduction to wig wear. It was glorious.

Yes, I put it on!

I looked like a star, a lead singer in a rock band; leather pants, studded vest, and handkerchiefs tied around the microphone stand. I could see it all in the platinum shag hairpiece resting atop my 12-year-old face.

The moment took control. I violently flung my head forward and back in a classic rock head banging move. The energy was too much for the loose-fitting wig. It launched off my head, soared across the room, and landed atop the lamp on the night stand. Ichabod's illuminated platinum hair glowed in a true rockstar tribute.

My attention turned to the reddish bob. Ichabod's brother needed an equally appropriate name. Scaribod.

Certainly, had anyone known what happened next, they would have sent me to therapy.

At certain stages of development, young boys can look like young girls and young girls can look like young boys. I was blessed, as it were, with a stunted development. In fact, masculine features, minus the scar, did not reign dominant until I was well into my 20s. Except for the genderization (again, should be a word) of hairstyles and clothing, boys and girls are basically the same. Where Ichabod's shag stirred dreams of stardom, the Scaribod's bob had an illicit allure. A soft natural feel.

I saw myself in the mirror with Scaribod's reddish bob on my non-gender specific face and didn't recognize myself. Scared by the rising feelings within me, I threw the wig off my head in a fit. The feelings didn't stop their rising. I was compelled to put the reddish bob back on.

It was one thing to dress like a cowboy or rockstar, those took the imagination, to be sure, but only so far. The reddish bob opened up a whole new realm of possibility. Mother's clothes were ill-fitting on me, but the results were still dramatic. I could be anybody, man or woman, in my own heaven of make believe. There was a sense of wholeness in the world of the reddish bob.

My apologies. I got lost in the fantastical past.

I tell you this story of Ichabod and Scaribod because I realized, in the approach to Mrs. McDermott, that I had a solution to my mustache problem. I stepped up to the counter, found the chapter on wigs in the Hollywood makeup book, folded the corner of its first page, closed the book, pushed it toward Mrs. McDermott, and said, "I don't need this book anymore, but it looks like you might."

At home, I rushed to my parents' bedroom. Too fast, unthinking, unprepared. I had not thought of my mother in some time. My father left everything the same. Her perfumes, brushes, photos, jewelry lay preserved, frozen in the motion of the day she left. I smelled the perfumes. Memories. My fingers ran over her favorite necklace. She left everything, took herself, and the clothes on her back. She must have had an emergency that drove her out unpacked. No time even to explain. Only a sparse note of goodbye. I lingered.

The platinum shag wig was in the exact place I had left it. I cut a mustache-sized piece off its backside. A black permanent marker took care of the color. I found a bottle of rubber cement in the kitchen's junk drawer. The pictures in the Hollywood makeup book showed ample glue. A loose mustache would serve nobody. I was generous in its application to my upper lip.

The rubber cement was aromatic in a pleasant, though intoxicating, way. Thankfully, it held the Ichabod mustache tightly to my lip. I remember a slight dizziness coming over me. I assumed it was from the overwhelming masculinity I felt as I looked at myself in the mirror.

I wouldn't say I fainted, but when I woke on the bathroom floor, I knew my life would, forever, be altered. Balthazar could hardly believe the transformation. He ran from me as I approached the corral. He probably thought I would take to manhandling him. I assured him I would use none of my newfound strength to harm him. Once satisfied with his safety, he was impressed and said as much in he repeated he was glad to finally have a proper partner with whom to walk through town.

I couldn't help but get lost in my newly found prowess. Domination, the goal of every man, was my destiny. The school yard was soon to be conquered. Every boy would move aside, fearing even the slightest provocation would unleash my man fury from which few would survive.

The headache, origins unknown, was not enough to dampen my excitement for school the next day. I slept like a baby; a strong, confident, and capable baby.

A new day had dawned. I was pleased. Heather was pleased. Balthazar was pleased.

I sprinted to the school bus stop nearly as soon as I woke.

6

ONCE REMOVED, TWICE BITTEN

A school bus has its own social structure and rules of engagement that don't relate to the real world. So when the snickers, whispers, and straight out name-calling began, I knew they hid all the kid's forbidden fear, insecurity, and genuine curiosity. A school bus is no place for vulnerability, Socratic inquiry, or pleasant attraction. No. Assumption, scorn, and unchallenged social order reign supreme on the school bus.

I think it was Plato who said, non colligunt pugna si nusquam currere. Don't pick a fight if you have nowhere to run.

Knowing this, I remained silent and impervious to the chaos. In twenty short and bumpy minutes, everything would change. Outside the protective bubble of the school bus number 509, the other kids would be defenseless against the manly virility of my mustache.

Someone, King James and Mr. Proverb I think it was, once said laughter was the best medicine. If the King was right, I healed an entire school's worth of students, teachers, and staff. So much healing through laughter had taken place by the end of the third period class that Principal Connor, sent word my presence was urgently needed in the front office. There must have been a sudden illness overcome the administrative staff for him to feel my studies could be delayed.

"Okay, Kid, everyone's had a nice laugh. It's time to take the mustache off," Principal Connor said.

"But, sir…"

He cut short my plea. "You, and that mustache, are a distraction that is disrupting the educational process for hundreds of students."

Finally, someone who had the self-confidence to acknowledge the truth, I was a threat to hundreds of students, I thought.

With a single prosthetic mustache, I had transformed my stature from gnat, easily squashed, to a raging bull trampling and goring villains and innocents alike. "Thank you, Principal Conner. Is there anything I can do for you. You know, to lighten your load."

"No son, seriously," he said, "take the mustache off."

There is no room for a prophet in his own land. No truer words were ever uttered.

Reluctantly, I opted for peace over violence. I was the stronger man. We both knew it. Better to have Principal Connor save face. He would remember my kindness in the future, I was sure.

I gave the mustache a sharp tug. A high-pitched wince emanated from somewhere near me. My upper lip immediately throbbed.

"Son, you need to remove the mustache, now. I'm not gonna ask again," Principal Connor said.

I took a gentle approach and attempted to peel back an edge. The folks at the rubber cement company sure knew a thing or two about adhesives. "A mustache, like love, is meant to last a lifetime," I said.

Mr. Connor wasn't impressed. The school nurse was

summoned. She tried both techniques I had previously employed which satisfied Principal Connor of my earnestness, but failed to remove my manliness.

Destiny has a way of survival. Darwinism on display.

She proclaimed to have done all she could and suggested that I try nail polish remover, of which she had none.

"For the good of the school, I am sending you home. You can return when the mustache is removed. And, don't take all day," Principal Connor said.

It was obvious that had I a little forethought, I could have predicted the debilitating power of a proper mustache. It was inconsiderate of me to endanger so many. I recommitted myself to the safety and wellbeing of my fellow man.

The hero must make sacrifices. On that day, I was forced to sacrifice my mustache for the greater good.

"What a shame, Kid. That's a right proper mustache," Reggie said.

"He looks handsome, doesn't he Heather?" Paul added.

Heather winked, "Too bad it has to go."

I found mother's supply of nail polish remover. Thankful that she left all her things. A guilty pang rose at the thought. Palm filled, I splashed it on my face, dousing the mustache. No sooner had I felt a queasiness than I woke on the bathroom floor.

Twice in one week. Strange.

The nail polish remover didn't do the trick. Obvious. Girl solvent for a man problem, I thought.

I went to the corral to consult with Balthazar. He was eager to help, "Put your forehead against the top rail of the fence."

This left the mustache exposed to him through the rail. He gripped Ichabod's mustache firmly between his teeth and violently shook his powerful neck left to right several times.

I never determined which caused the blackout, my forehead

striking the fence rail several times or the searing pain from my upper lip. I woke lying flat on my back. Balthazar proudly proclaimed his success. A doctor should have been called about the sudden onset of fainting that had befallen me but I had more pressing issues.

The bleeding stopped in time for dinner and, though tender and slightly loose, my teeth were functioning. The scab that formed by the morning resembled the Ichabod mustache.

"You better stay home for a few days. You know, for the good of the other students," Heather said.

The additional rest eased the fainting. Not enough time for lip healing.

Duty called as did the school. Principal Connor would certainly send me home as soon as he saw me. Lucky for me, a family emergency kept him home. This gave my classmates a chance to congratulate and celebrate my accomplishments. It was evident that my healing gesture earlier in the week elicited a kind and welcoming nature that I always knew existed in the kids.

Their gift of gratitude?

One of their prized possessions. A suave nickname.

Not lightly given but they could hardly contain their enthusiasm. By lunchtime the whole school called me, Stache.

Stache.

That was a noble name. It was right up there with John Wayne's, The Duke. Annie Oakley's, Little Miss Sure Shot. Wilt The Stilt Chamberlain. Andre The Giant. Ivan The Terrible. Smokin' Joe Fraser. Hector Macho Camacho. And, Ray Boom Boom Mancini.

The pain in my upper lip vanished.

The adults were less grateful. Their refusal to call me Stache, I knew, was a reaction to the threat I posed as an equal. Kids respect strength. They honor accomplishment. Adults invent ways to subvert both.

I would deal with the elderly another day. This moment with my peers was to be savored. For the first time in a long time, I smiled. The mustache worked. A gnarly scar and a fanciful nickname. Mere waypoints on a man's man journey. Hard earned as they were, I knew a man's destiny, my destiny, lay written in red lipstick on a bathroom mirror.

7

SUBSTANCE MAKES THE MAN

Becoming a man, a true man's man, is not for everyone. Maybe not even for me. A nasty scar on my forehead and a disfigured upper lip were the only indications of my journey. Each a testament to manhood's contradiction wherein success and failure look the same.

Balthazar often quoted himself, saying, "Substantia facit hominem. Stultus sola specie ducitur." Substance makes the man. A fool is guided by appearance alone.

My reflection and the man-making list stared back at me in the mirror. I read aloud the list. "Get mustache." I felt better in an instant. I struck a line of lipstick through this one. On a roll. "Which to tackle next?" I asked aloud.

"Get tall." I stood on the step stool next to the sink. I looked for inspiration. None arrived.

"Get muscles." I raised my arms and flexed in a classic strong man pose. Nothing. I placed my left fist behind my right bicep and smashed it against my rib cage. Nothing still.

"Smoke cigarettes." I practiced with my toothbrush. Possibilities.

"Be an Athlete." Too much to consider. I rationalized.

"Be brave and courageous." Odysseus of Homer's Odyssey had a scar from his wild boar hunt when he was a teenager. He returned from the hunt no longer a boy. Right of passage, man stuff. I studied my scar. My attempt to save the town was my hunt. Magnus Mendacium my boar. I relished in my accomplishment. Scars gotten through the hunt, battle, or adventure are marks of honor. I scratched through Brave and Courageous with the lipstick. Substance meets appearance.

"Be a ladies' man. Did I like girls?" I asked myself. I wasn't sure whether I did or didn't. A matter of consideration more than desire. I simply had not thought about the subject. Thinking for another day.

"Get dirty." Several days had passed since my last shower. I raised the lipstick to mark a line through. Hesitation. Getting dirty and being dirty are two different things, I thought. I was dirty for laziness and neglect, not intent. Action and effort. Can't take credit where credit isn't due.

"Get in a fight and win." I grimaced at my own reflection and threw a few punches in the air. That felt good. I went harder. My shoulder erupted in pain. Too strong even for my own body. I vowed to take it easy on myself and others. More possibilities.

Overall, this was a strange way to judge myself. I examined me for the man in me. The scar, according to Heather was manly. Unsightly to me. The disfigured upper lip, unsettling. The lipstick was a cleaver distraction but it was temporary. I could never go outside with Le Rouge St. Germaine. Tempting but no. Girls got all the fun stuff.

The lingering lip pain was a constant reminder even without the mirror. The truth was I did not feel very manly in that moment. It had nothing to do with the lipstick. I felt less interested in the remaining man-making items on the list. I conquered the two most exciting, saving the town and the prosthetic mustache.

I wiped off the lipstick and headed out to feed Balthazar. Perfect timing. He had a craving. It was my fault, really. After the mustache incident, he took to accompanying me most places, most days, including school. He spent the day in the pasture out back of the gym building. The field's owner didn't seem to mind and Balthazar never overindulged.

One afternoon, I introduced him to Custard's Last Stand: Homemade Ice Creams and Sodas, the town's only ice cream shop. He insisted on a vanilla cone for himself. One cone, his first cone, and he was an addict. We liked Custard's on account of the walk-up order window and its ample outdoor seating. Balthazar didn't feel crowded.

He finished his morning rations and announced his need for vanilla cone. One of my more enterprising classmates had taken to selling pictures of me. With me, more specifically. She even built a backdrop. One dollar got her customer a photo with

Stache. She gave me $.25 for each picture taken. When he was in the mood, Balthazar posed for photos. Those were two dollars. Balthazar negotiated $.75 per photo for himself. The point was that Balthazar had plenty of money to pay for ice cream anytime he had a craving. He usually paid for mine also. So, there was no doubt we were going for ice cream that afternoon.

To watch a horse eat an ice cream cone was quite a sight. My record for least number of bites to finish a single scoop ice cream cone was ten. Balthazar's was one. One bite and gone. His was less of a record than a habit. Rarely did he take two bites. He had, once, set a record for number of cones in one sitting. Six, one after another. Six bites, six cones, one serious freeze headache. He never tried to top this record.

Balthazar tended to make friends anywhere we went. At Custard's he befriended Josh and Tyler, two eleven year-old boys who liked ice cream as much as we did. The two of them took to Balthazar as much as Balthazar had taken to them. They liked to pull on his mane, rub his belly, and pretend to ride him.

On this particular afternoon of Balthazar's craving, he had two cones and patiently waited for me to finish my one. A patch of grass behind Custard's Last Stand caught his attention. He was off and missed the ruckus.

I busily shaped and trimmed my scoop of Butter Scotch Ripple with my tongue in an effort to eliminate unwelcome drips. I had a keen sixth sense as a child. Whether I subconsciously hoped to see Josh and Tyler or my sixth sense was active, my attention was drawn away from my cone. I looked up just as the bully, Bradford "The Bull" Bartells, pushed Josh to the ground. The Bull and his sidekick, Robbie "The Rototiller" Evans, struck a menacing stance over my two young friends.

I heard Tyler say, "You can't have our money and you better not touch him again."

"And what are you going to do about it, little boy," The Bull said.

A vision of me, face-to-face with Stevie Fester and the rest of the bully squad on the first day of school flashed into my head.

I heard Tyler's words and my body surged with an anger I never knew existed in me. I dropped the cone as I ran to the scene and thrust my body between Tyler and The Bull.

8

THE BULL SLAYER

To insert oneself into another man's fight is a dangerous act. Each of us has to walk our own journey. I could have just as easily been stealing Tyler and Josh's victory as I was saving their lives. In the heat of battle, there is little room for such considerations. These are the luxuries of hindsight. In that moment, I had no idea what possessed me. I wasn't any bigger than Josh and Tyler. The thought of danger and my own demise didn't enter my mind. A warrior's instinct driving his actions.

I was surely going to be pummeled by The Bull. Better me than Tyler and Josh, I thought. The harsh reality of heroism.

I squared up with The Bull and puffed out my chest. He scoffed and Robbie laughed at my bravado. The Bull stood his ground. So much for my bluff. This was going to get physical. May the gods of heaven and earth have mercy on our souls for surely this would be a dual to the death, I thought.

The Bull cranked his right arm back in a classic haymaker stance. I'd seen this in the movies many times. I simply had to step back or duck, let the punch sail by harmlessly, and then spring in action. I couldn't decide my best move, duck or step back, nor could I think which counterstrike to employ. I felt myself freeze up. The sense that this would end poorly set in.

My vision was tunneled in its heightened state and focused on The Bull. I had not seen that Balthazar had snuck up on the scene. Just as Bradford set to release his haymaker, Balthazar clamped down on his jacket collar. Based on the screaming, I imagined Balthazar had a mouthful of The Bull's shoulder also. The Bull rose off the ground and dangled from Balthazar's teeth. Robbie, initially startled by the site, had regained himself and was about to lunge at Balthazar, both fists blazing. Josh, who had remained on the ground through the entire confrontation, crawled on all fours and positioned himself behind Robbie's legs. I unleashed my fury into the midsection of The Rototiller. He never saw it coming. Josh's body formed an effective fulcrum against Robbie's legs. Robbie's upper body had no choice, but to slam hard against the curb. Balthazar shook The Bull left to right several times releasing him mid-air to land in a heap on top of Robbie.

Balthazar reared back on his hind legs and came down hard on his front hooves missing Bradford and Robbie's heads by inches. He lowered his face to theirs and released a nasal clearing snort.

I have known fear my entire life. One might say, I have an active and intimate relationship with fear. And yet, I don't think I have felt a fear as intensely as the one I saw on Robbie and Bradford's faces. They sprang to their feet and sprinted down the road. Balthazar galloped loudly on their heels for several blocks.

He arrived back at Custard's Last Stand to cheers and hugs from all of the customers. None were more grateful than Josh and Tyler. The manager came out to greet Balthazar with two vanilla cones. "On the house," he proudly announced.

Word spread throughout town pretty fast. Our walk home

took twice as long as usual as people came out of their shops and homes or stopped their cars in the middle of the street to get a hug and scratch the neck of Balthazar. I had a brave and strong friend. The town had it's hero. I secretly hoped some of that would rub off on me.

At home, I regaled Heather and the others in our exploits. She was impressed. They were impressed. She suggested that I could strike through getting in a fight and winning. "One step closer to your man," she said.

I wasn't convinced. Technically, Balthazar had done most of the actual fighting. Josh, Tyler, and I assisted. The victory was Balthazar's. Credit where credit is due.

Besides my vision for my man fight was of a mano-a-mano, man-to-man, one-on-one match. My day would come.

The rest of the weekend did nothing to diminish the town's enthusiasm. Word had spread through the entire school. Monday there was a steady stream of kids in the pasture behind the school to touch Balthazar, "The Bull Slayer". That was a fine nickname.

At lunch, I had taken my usual spot at the far end of the cafeteria. Alone. This was my habit. Better to give the others their space. I was surprised to look up from my French toasted bacon sandwich to see Bethany Baumgardner standing over me. Bethany was in the in crowd. She might've been the ringleader of the in crowd. I didn't pay much attention to such matters other than she always had a crew of girls and boys trailing and circling around her.

I looked left and right, clearly she was lost.

"Stache," she said. "I can call you Stache, right?"

"I guess so." I was off to good start for my first interaction with the school's royalty. I eased into a casual slouch under the lunch room table.

"I want to thank you for stepping in and helping my little

brother, Josh. He said you stood up for him and his friend, Tyler."

"That was really Balthazar who did that. He's out back if you wanna talk to him."

"Well, according to Josh and Tyler, it was you who stepped in between them and The Bull and you pushed Robbie down to the ground. That was very brave. Nobody ever stands up to those bullies. And you did."

"I don't know about that."

"I do and you did just that. You are kind of a hero, you know. The whole school is talking about it."

I fell into a daydream of me entering the Hall of Justice for a meeting of the Superheroes. My cape fluttering in my wake.

"Stache? Stache!" Bethany prodded. "So, anyway, I just wanted to say thanks. You're an okay kid in my eyes."

"Oh, 'em, so are you." I was really on my game. I leaned hard into the slouch to express an air of cool kid vibe.

"Okay, then. I'll see you around, Stache," Bethany said as she stood up from the table.

After school, I found Balthazar surrounded by a pack of kids. Trapped. Fifty hands petting and patting him. I called for him but he was paralyzed. I reached for the apple in my backpack. He let out a neigh, followed by a light snort, and shake of his head. The kids scattered with a collective shriek. The Bull Slayer, indeed.

On our walk home, I told him what Bethany had said.

"Becoming a man," Balthazar said, "involves the assumption of the divine powers of goodness, wisdom, strength, compassion, resilience, and purpose."

More riddles.

I suddenly longed for the bygone days of Homer, Odysseus, and the hunt. Odysseus had one item on his man list. Kill wild boar. He did it and became a man. "Life has gotten complicated in the modern world," I said.

Balthazar was unmoved by my musings. "It was enough that you faced your fear. In this case, a bully, and stood firm in spite of certain defeat. It wasn't for yourself, for a victory, or for your man-making quest that you stood up. It was for your friends. And that was a noble act. An act worthy of a man."

Back in the bathroom, I examined the list and my reflection in the mirror. Get in Fight and Win, a well-deserved red lipstick line through it.

Substantia facit hominem. Substance makes the man.

A MAN IS AS A MAN DOES

Still a boy. Still on a quest to be a man. The dark and lonely days of a long journey.

My man-making had stagnated as the fanfare of the fight with The Bull wore off. Proving my man required a daily reaffirmation of the previously established facts. No 'one and done' in the man-making department. Time for rejuvenation. Time to talk to Balthazar.

Two pitchforks full of hay and a scoop of oats. Balthazar was ready to impart his wisdom.

"Heraclitus said, 'Mille advenis dulces non sunt pertemptant viae unires sine fine.' One thousand sweet arrivals is not worth the thrill of a single endless journey."

Riddles. Heather will know what to do, I thought.

"Opportunity, like hope, springs eternal," Heather said. "If you are ever lost or stuck in life, the fantastical will bring you home. Set your gaze toward Hollywood."

Wisdom I could use.

Books, and movies by extension, exist for this reason. Examples of adventure, morality, manliness, womanliness, and courage are rarely found in one person. Even rarer, is for that one person to be near you as you grow up. We need books. We need movies. We need stories told a thousand different ways to incite our imagination, beliefs, and behaviors.

My imagination was titillated by the Saturday afternoon television show about movie stunts and the stuntmen and stunt-women who performed them. They were the real deal. The show was an informative, step-by-step, tutorial for those of us outside of Hollywood. It should have been mandatory learning in school like the four weeks of health stuff during gym class.

Turns out the real men of Hollywood had other, more real, more manly, men who fought the fights, crashed the cars, and jumped off the cliffs. The stuntman. Reality and fiction blended to guide my way.

I was compelled to re-create a western movie scene in which the outlaws were on one side of the riverbank and the lawman on the other. Each shooting at one another. One outlaw, out of ammunition, called to his partner to toss him a loaded rifle. The rifle thrown, suspended above the river, awaited the outlaw's grasp. He launched himself from his covered position on the riverbank. Just as he reached the rifle he was shot by the lawmen. The impact of the bullet drove his body back onto the embankment. Dead.

High drama to be sure.

The behind the scenes stuntman show revealed the intricate details of the elaborate and effective stunt. I was convinced the actor was shot. Not so. The stuntman who stood in for the actor had a rope tied around his waist. When he leapt for the rifle, three of his friends yanked the rope as hard as they could. Magnificent.

Our house sat along a dry creek bed. My riverbank. I needed a yanker. Balthazar was my best hope as Heather and the others didn't get out much. Balthazar was in a particularly cheerful mood and volunteered to assist.

My plan was simple, yet, well-conceived. We reviewed the details several times. I reinforced the safety protocols just like the stuntmen.

I tied one end of the rope around Balthazar's neck and the other around my waist. We positioned ourselves with our backs to one another. Me near the edge of the riverbank and him facing toward the yard. We left six feet of slack in the rope. As far as plans goes, I thought the elegance of this one spoke to a genius within.

Three feet to the edge. Three feet to soar through the air toward the rifle. Balthazar would feel the rope tighten and bolt toward the yard and I would land in a dramatic Hollywood death scene, unharmed, at the edge of the cliff. Oats and apples awaited our success.

As I took a final breath before yelling action, it dawned on me that there was real danger in what I was about to do. No real stuntman training. I watched a T.V. show. Images of me in the middle of Main Street with dad's Colt .45 revolver flashed into my mind. The scar began to throb. Was this the same mistake? I mused. What did I know about rope knots. Was this a knot that would unravel at the slightest of tugs? How old was the rope? Would it hurt to hit the ground?

I was just a kid. A boy. Not a man. Certainly not a man's man. Not a stuntman.

Balthazar looked at me with an encouraging snort. A good omen. His intuition was unassailable. His confidence bolstered my own.

As if by divine intervention an Aristotle quote appeared in my mind. "There is no great genius without some touch of madness."

"Action," I yelled.

A sprint to the edge. A dive toward the rifle. This must be what a bird feels like, I thought. The rope tightened around my waist. A powerful force snatched my body violently backward. In preparation for landing on the riverbank, my arms and legs splayed out in an imagined death. My body slumped into the embankment. Hollywood performance par excellence.

Balthazar must have misunderstood the scene's direction.

The impact with the ground knocked the air out of my lungs. No audible sounds from my mouth despite my attempts to yell "cut" or "scene", or anything. My body continued to bounce across the ground. It occurred to me that directors and stuntmen often use marks on the set to indicate start and stop locations. Balthazar could have benefited from a marker to remind him that he was to take only a few steps. Three feet. One gallop. A proverbial skip and hop for a horse.

Balthazar was in a full sprint. I, in a full panic.

I needed to regain directorial control over my crew. The dust kicked up by Balthazar's hooves and my flailing body filled my lungs as I gasped for air. The mercy of the gods was all I had left.

They came through.

Balthazar was more of an intellectual than a sportsman. He tired after half a lap around the yard. He beamed at his performance. I couldn't deny he executed near flawlessly. Clearly, the failure to set a mark was my oversight.

No harm done. I found my pants with little effort. It was tricky and icky but I managed to remove the small pebbles and not an insignificant amount of dirt from parts we shouldn't mention in mixed company.

"Surviving is thriving," Heather says.

The show must go on. In this case, with a revised plan.

For my second attempt, I placed the rope in Balthazar's

mouth. He was to give a yank of his mighty neck. It worked with the prosthetic mustache. Fewer moving parts and a solid track record.

Repositioned, I crouched at the ready to hurl myself toward stardom, "Action," I yelled.

10

FRIENDS CAN BE FUN

As I soared through the air, I could hear the gunfire and feel the bullets whirl overhead. The rifle was within reach. The bullet struck me dead center of my chest. A kill shot to be sure. I had a split second to make peace with my maker before my body would crash against the riverbank in a lifeless heap.

It was my fault really. I should have looked at Balthazar before I yelled action. Had I done so, I would have seen that he had gotten an itch on his left hip. He dropped the rope to bite at the source of his discomfort. Any of us would have done the same.

My body, fully alive, continued unabated from the cliff's edge. I say cliff's edge because this was an ancient riverbed carved in sandy soil. I was suddenly falling twenty-five feet with no tension on the rope to slow my descent. Fortune had it such that two thirds to the bottom, the cliff turned to a slope of loose grained sand. I slid and tumbled to the dry bed, unharmed. The full length of the rope cascaded down on top of me.

Minor inconvenience. As was the trek back home.

Balthazar was both excited and shocked to see me trailing a

waft of dust and the rope. "One minute you were there, the next, both you and the rope, gone," he explained.

Although determined to try again, Balthazar had his doubts.

"Hey. Can I try?" An unexpected voice. I turned.

It was Dill. He lived close by. Same age. Same School. Since kindergarten. A lot of sames. Despite the similarities, we never developed a friendship. Probably because he was kind of sickly and missed a lot of school. It's not that we were not friendly just not chums. Dill wasn't his real name either. He got his nickname in the third grade on account of how his mother had packed him a pickle for lunch every day since kinder. He must've really liked pickles. Nine years of pickles that I knew of at the time.

It didn't let up. But that's for another time.

Dill explained that he saw me jump off the cliff. His initial worry abated as I emerged hauling the rope. He figured he had to get in on the action. I told him of how I was re-creating the scene from the western movie.

"I'll be the yanker," he said. "But you have to yank me back."

From the vantage point of a fifteen year old boy at the onset of a man quest, false bravado can carry you far.

I handed the yanking end of the rope to Dill. He took up his position near where Balthazar had stood. I positioned myself as I had on the prior jump. I looked back this time. Dill was prepared.

"Action," I yelled.

Just as twice before, I arrived within reach of the rifle only to be shot in the chest. I felt a tug on the rope followed immediately by a slack in the rope.

Dill lost his footing. What followed was a slow motion dragging of Dill down the cliff face. I landed at the dry creek bed. Dill tumbled down behind me, rope in hand. His body crashed on top of mine.

Unharmed, we both had a great laugh.

"Let's do it again," he said.

We climbed out of the dry river bed. I tied the rope around his waist and grabbed the loose end. We took our positions.

"Action," he yelled.

I gave the rope a good yank as he launched off the cliff. Immediately, I felt myself lurch toward the cliff, tumble over the edge, cascade down, and land in a heap nearly on top of Dill.

There is a physics theorem that says if two kids of equal weight oppose one another, the kid with the greatest momentum will pull the other off a cliff. I am paraphrasing.

Fun as this was for both of us, we failed to deliver a man's man result. We needed Hollywood level action and precision. Any 'ol boy could tumble off a cliff. A man, however, would reach the rifle and save his buddies or die trying.

The path to the imprimatur of man lay in a total commitment of heart and soul. And other body parts.

The thrill of the journey had arrived.

And with Dill as my witness and me as his, our victory would be a triumphant embrace of camaraderic (I know, not a word, but should be) bond of man-ness having saved one another from our meek and soft-skinned existence.

First, we needed a revised plan. In a moment of brilliance, Balthazar suggested we tie one end of the rope to a tree.

"Run as fast as you can away from the tree. It will pull you right back," he said.

His confidence was contagious.

The rope cinched smoothly around the tree. I ran without a smidge of doubt as to the result or my safety. The tension caught me. I was yanked, arms and legs out in front of me, backward toward the tree. I landed on my buttocks, unarmed, and triumphant.

Dill was exuberant. His results were equally magnificent.

Hollywood action. Real stuntman stuff.

At this point in my young life, I was unaware of the organ system of the body. I suppose, had I paid attention in that gym health class, I would've known a thing or two about the spleen. I hadn't and was unaware of its location or purpose. That was, until Josh and Tyler showed up at my house.

Dill and I had perfected the rope and tree stunt and we're about to go inside for a snack when they arrived. We gave them a full briefing, including the safety protocols. They volunteered to give it a try.

Each one flawless. On Tyler's third run, all appeared normal except for the screams of pain and anguish.

Time for that snack break.

Unknown to me, Dill was quite a cook. He had spent a lot of time on his own learning the art. "Because I like to eat," he said. He made us grilled cheese sandwiches with garlic, salt, and oregano. A pickle on the side, of course.

Regarding Tyler, he enjoyed the grilled cheese sandwich, but continued to hold his abdomen. We tended to his possible injury with chocolate milk and a butterscotch pudding cup.

It wasn't enough. He went home.

11

KNOWLEDGE THROUGH ADVERSITY
AND, AT TIMES, INJURY

I saw Josh the next Saturday at Custard's Last Stand. He said Tyler was at home recovering from surgery. His mother, unconvinced of our medical interventions, took him to the hospital.

Apparently, a spleen can rupture given enough force from a rope around the mid-section.

Tyler was back to stunt-manning soon enough. The four of us spent Saturdays at my house where we watched the stuntman show and recreated the scenes. Tyler's spleen mishap sharpened our focus on safety.

For the car rollover stunt, we selected an steeply inclined road with a shoulder of soft dirt and a grassy embankment. Josh's peddle car was perfect even without the roll cage that the stuntmen had in theirs. We roped two pillows around our shoulders to cushion the fall. Helmets not required.

On the T.V., we watched the stuntmen fall from a tall building into an air mattress that deflated when they landed. We didn't have either. We did have a house surrounded by a recently plowed field. Our version of the tall building and soft landing.

Some stunts took real creativity to pull off. Dill proved

himself smart in these matters. We didn't have cables with which to suspend ourselves in the air for the Superman flying scenes. Dill rigged several large garbage bags to our backs, like a parachute. The makeshift parachute would fill with air as we reached a certain speed on the skateboard and lift us off the ground. Under our own power, we hadn't a chance. Not enough speed. A down hill run filled the parachute but failed to create the loft. In our final attempt, Superman was pulled on a skateboard by one of us riding a bike.

Success.

A few scrapped and sprained limbs were small prices for the elation that accompanied the attempts and their successes. This was my first recollection of being lost in ideas and adventure. Of time and space blended. Of friendship and mutual admiration. The thrill in the journey.

Ingenuity + invention + intention = fun with friends.

We experimented. We took risks. We actioned in the face of fear. We persevered. We bonded through pain. Dill, Tyler, Josh, and I, shared a stuntman's courage.

A side benefit for me was that Dill spent a lot of time at my house. He was quite a fine fellow. Aside from stunt-manning, he mostly liked food and cooking. You wouldn't know this by looking at him. He looked like me, well by size anyway. He taught me to cook lots of meals. Oatmeal with raisins, cinnamon, and vanilla ice cream. Canned tuna sandwiches with boiled eggs, finely chopped pickles, onions, paprika, salt, and pepper. Omelette with fresh dill, no surprise, goat cheese, and bacon. Dill had a problem with cow cheese but apparently goats didn't bother him. He invented new recipes for us to try. His creativity made him invaluable to our stuntman work.

He told me that he wasn't really sickly. He just didn't like to go to school. The school part, reading, math, and such, he liked. He was good at the school parts. Real smart. Smarter than me.

The other stuff. The other kids. They were a riddle for which he had no solution. He was fond of saying, "School would be great if it weren't for all these kids."

He must've been an old soul.

I noticed one day, as I stared out the window lost in a daydream during history class, that Dill was there. Not only was he there that day, he had been there the previous day. In fact, I couldn't remember the last time he had missed school.

I didn't mind. I liked the company at lunch. Dill even talked now and then with the other kids. A couple of times a week, Bethany would come talk to us at lunch. She would say how Josh was so excited about a stunt we had done or the food we made. I didn't understand the fuss. We knew Josh had a good time. We were there with him.

All this to say, strange things were happening. The people around me were...happy. I resisted the distraction of solving this mystery. Exploration for another day.

I had man-making to do. The list was in the mirror, staring back at me. It pierced my psyche.

I consulted Heather.

"Dreams are no substitute for the doing," she said.

I went to Balthazar. "Nisi per facere potest habere scienticiam. Only through doing can one have knowledge," he said.

Heather spoke in riddles and Balthazar in tongues.

Doing was my problem. What to do? How to do it? Not as a boy but as a man.

Doing as a horse does was easy for Balthazar. He was everything a horse was supposed to be. Noble, independent, confident. Similarly for Heather. Being a superstar came easy for her. She just was.

Heather brought the discussion back to the list. "All can dream," she said. "Fewer do. My father used to say, 'The hardest bolt you will ever turn is the first bolt you ever turn.' To experience for yourself the stunts from the television show, was doing."

"She is right," Gene chimed in. "You show us everything you've got. You keep on dancing till the room gets hot."

Song lyrics? I got it, he speaks in song lyrics.

I needed to talk to Balthazar.

"I was sure that stuntman business would be the death of you," he said. "But look what it has done. Dill hadn't missed a day of school in weeks. You are walking taller. The stuntman stunts, the friendship, and the actions of living are impacting your lives. Everything in nature can only be what it is by doing what it does. Allow yourself to become as you do."

I went back to the bathroom mirror.

It dawned on me that my last shower was a week ago. Too long for the finery of civilized living but about right for a manly man's life. I was dirty through action not laziness.

Progress.

I crossed through get dirty with Le Rouge St. Germaine and jumped into the shower.

12

LADIES' MEN

My victories, as marked by the red lipstick felt fraudulent. Time to rectify. Time to be deterministic. Time to man up. I explained this to Balthazar.

Balthazar rolled his eyes, muttered, "Oh boy." and returned to his oats.

He didn't understand the stakes nor appreciate the depth of my determination. "I failed to grab the reins. Failed to drive toward a man-making action item on the list," I said.

"Would you rather be lucky or smart?" Balthazar said.

Riddles.

"Lying docile while the situations of life ruled over my actions is like a weighted blanket on my chest."

I was no cabin boy on the steamship of my life. I was the Captain.

I was no houseboy of my castle. I was the King.

Time to chart a course to far away lands and subjugate the masses.

Time to review the list.

Socrates said, "Speculum non mentior." A mirror cannot lie.

Standing at the mirror, I found solace in Socrates' truth. My reflection incited joy where it had previously sparked a shame of inadequacy. I couldn't help but admit that I looked rather dashing in Le Rouge St. Germain. Who wouldn't really?

The list? Of course, the list.

Get Mustache; check. Get Dirty; check. Be Brave and Courageous; check. Get in Fight and Win; check.

The memories of adventure flooded my mind. I risked life and limb to warn the town of approaching danger. The entire school bathed in the healing power of laughter. The bully squad had cowered in the face of superior intellect and skill. Lifelong bonds were forged through action and adversity and together we elevated our man-making journeys.

Earlier feelings of fraudulence dissipated. Confidence bolstered. Resolve fueled. I read aloud the remaining list.

Get Taller.

Be a Ladies' Man.

Get Muscles.

Be an Athlete.

Smoke Cigarettes.

I could've easily made a rash decision. I resisted. My indecision should not be seen as an indication of dampened enthusiasm. The thing of it was that Heather had been instrumental in creating the list. I knew she would want to be included in the deliberation.

"Which one scares you the most?" She asked.

Silly girls with silly questions, I thought

I was a stuntman with scars of valor and a manly nickname. Scared? Fear played no role in the movie of my life. It wasn't fear that made my fingers numb, that made my stomach tingle, or that took my breath away. No, when I read Be A Ladies' Man, it was the excitement of the hunt. The anticipation of victory. The visions of future adoration. Those were the thoughts that paralyzed me.

Suave. The right words always at the tip of the tongue. Ready to swoon. The dress, the hair, the stature, the confidence, the eyes. Lady killer. Hollywood's leading man.

If I had a fear, it was based on how unprepared my peers were for the full release of the ladies' man within me. Prepared or not, I had my mission.

"I think you have your answer," she said.

Yes I did. I wiped off the lipstick and sprinted out the front door.

Dill was already at the corral. "Welcome to the first day of the rest of your life," he said. This was his daily greeting. He started each day fresh and free from the burdens of the past, he explained. This allowed him to see unlimited possibilities ahead of him.

His optimism never wavered. Today, I needed a shot of his passion for potential.

"How are we going to change our stars today?" He asked.

"Today we are ladies' men."

"Ladies?"

"Ladies!" I said. "Welcome to the first day of the rest of your life."

Dill remained silent for most of the walk to school. Contemplating how spectacular the rest of his life would be, no doubt.

"Stache, I have been thinking about this ladies' man stuff."

"Yes, exciting, isn't it?"

"Well, seems like we might have to meet people. Like girl people. I am not so good at that."

An obvious feign of uncertainty. I could sense his unspoken enthusiasm and I knew that he had to offer at least one objection. A common tactic employed by confident men.

"Not at all, Dill. Being a ladies' man only requires the two of us."

"What about the ladies?"

"They take care of themselves. Think about all the classics. Humphrey Bogart in Casablanca. Clark Gable in Gone With The Wind. James Dean in Giant. Steve McQueen in... anything. Paul Newman in Cool Hand Luke. They were debonair and rakish. The ladies just came to them."

"Debonair?"

His resistance was evaporating under the searing rays of hope I offered.

"Confident, poised, witty, slow to talk, fast to action. The marks of a ladies' man," I said. "Today, they will be our marks."

Balthazar left us at the entrance to the school. He chuckled to himself as he rounded the corner toward the field. Something tickled his funny bone on our walk, I thought.

Buoyed by our spirited conversation, Dill headed to the nurse's office. "My stomach hurts," he said.

I went to my locker. Locker number 981, mine, sat at the midpoint of Corridor F in Building D. The entrance to the building opened onto Corridor A which served as a spine of sorts. Subsequent corridors were right and left offshoots of the main one. F, my corridor, was at the lonely and opposite end of the primary doors. This main hallway, as you might imagine from my lengthy description, was a foreboding gauntlet to be traversed numerous times daily.

"Everything happens for a reason," Heather often said.

Today, thanks in part, to Balthazar's and Dill's reassuring confidence, Corridor A lay before me as a stage. A playland through which to strut my ladies' man. The door opened with ease. Eyes squinted. Chin, forward. Corner of mouth, upturned. Shoulders, squared. Chest, forward. Posed and poised. I breezed across the threshold.

13

NOT YOUR GRANDFATHER'S LADY'S MAN

My presence was arresting. Corridor A came to an abrupt halt. Thirty kids in the immediate area were stupefied by my magnificence.

You can imagine the shock for all of us when the door handle made violent contact with my backside. None more so than Lindsay Jo Callahan. She walked, at an unnecessarily rapid pace, toward the same door I had just entered through when my arrival caused her to pause. In her arms were two text books, a three-ringed binder, a spiral notebook, a pencil case, and an untold number of personal care items. A backpack would have relieved us of a lot of trouble.

However, that being said, my presence undoubtedly saved her life for she would surely have met an untimely demise at the handle of the door. As I careened through the air toward Lindsay Jo, I felt like a Secret Service Agent diving in front of a bullet destined for the President. Her shield from the unseen door danger. Any ladies' man would have done the same. The rest of what unfolded was pure man instinct. My short but effective shriek gave her an instant to cast her books aside and allow me to guide her body gently to the floor.

"Stache!" She yelled. "What are you doing?"

In the tumble to the floor, I ended up on top of Lindsay Jo. Face-to-face. Up close, her features seemed exaggerated or perhaps I had never noticed how open her pores were or the amount of fuzz she had along her cheek or that her left eyebrow was considerably thicker than her right. One cannot truly know another until you get nice and close to them. I enjoyed this moment to get to know Lindsay Jo but alas we couldn't just lay there all day. Pushing myself off her, careful to not touch places a gentlemen should not touch, I deepened my voice and pronounced my assessment of the situation.

"I am doing the only thing I know to do, ma'am," I said.

"Ma'am?"

"Your life was in peril by this malfunctioning door. I placed myself between you and certain harm. My sacrifice for your safety."

"Stache, are you right in the head?"

"The head is great. My backside a bit sore. But a small price to pay. Allow me to assist with the gathering of your items."

It was heartening to me that the healing power of laughter was enveloping the surrounding mass of kids. My presence was needed, of this, I had no doubt. In an effort to mimic my selflessness, several kids gathered Lindsay Jo's books and supplies before I had an opportunity to do so.

"Well, there you go now, Lindsay Jo. Rest assured I will be reporting the malfunctioning door to Principal Connor and Mr. Grady," I said. Mr. Grady was the head janitor and a personal acquaintance of mine. I dare say, friend. My locker was next to his supply closet so we saw one another often.

The remaining walk to Corridor F was slow on account of the sharp pain erupting in my backside with each stride. Seemed that lifting my leg was causing a relapse of my recent injury. By the time lunch rolled around, I had perfected the shuffle step.

Dill waited for me at our usual spot in the cafeteria.

I lowered myself into the bench across from him.

"Stache, I don't think I am cut out to be a ladies' man," he said.

"Too late, you already are a ladies' man."

"Nurse Hamilton said I am too young to be thinking about such things and I should avoid stressful thoughts as they upset my stomach."

"Dill, you are a stuntman. Stuntmen are ladies' men. They are inseparable like a pickle to a sandwich."

"I see."

"Take me, for instance. This morning, my body, without a thought in my mind, simply placed itself between Lindsay Jo Callahan and a malfunctioning door. Real ladies' man work."

"Some kids were talking about that in geography class. They said you pushed her to the floor."

"Had to. Couldn't risk her getting hurt."

"Yeah, but it looks like you got hurt."

"Think about it, Dill. We hurt when we do stuntman work. We hurt when we do ladies' man work. A working man just hurts. That's how it is."

"You sure there isn't a better way?"

Dill knew how to ask the tough questions.

Given the success of my first day of ladies' man work, I put off thinking about this until after school.

Though Balthazar agreed that riding him home would be quicker, he felt that walking off the pain of my earlier conquests would be more therapeutic. "Besides," he said, "it's not far to Custard's Last Stand. My treat."

This day was just getting better and better.

Tyler and Josh arrived shortly after we did.

"Hey there, Stache. Hey, Dill," they both said.

"My sister said you tackled Lindsay Jo Callahan to the ground before school today," Josh said.

Good news travels fast in a small town.

"Tackled? No. Saved? Yes," I said. The conversation quickly turned to more pressing matters of stuntman activities. I enjoyed the respite from the more complicated aspects of being a man.

Dill's question loomed heavy.

A better way? I laid awake in bed with the question. Images of Bogart, Gable, Dean, McQueen, and Newman danced in my mind. They were near perfect representations of their time. The dress, the hair, the speak. My time wasn't their time. I could learn from them but I could not imitate them. I needed to be a perfect representation of my time.

Starchild spoke. "You have Ichabod's platinum hair."

"Calling Dr. Love," Gene sang.

I know that song, I thought. "That just might work," I said.

Balthazar had his answer. I would rather be lucky than smart. A perfectly flawless plan was forming. A better way, to be sure.

14

DRESSED TO KILL, ROCKER STYLE

Ichabod hadn't moved. The missing mustache sized swatch didn't distract from the drama of the moment.

"The ladies' men of today are the rockers," Heather said. She had an affinity for a certain drummer of a superstar rock band.

Gene, Paul, Ace, and Eric agreed. "We will help you with your makeup and outfit," they said.

I had the lipstick. The eyeliner, mascara, and eye shadow were easily found in my mother's left behind makeup case.

Again, strangely grateful she departed in a hurry.

At the bottom of my dresser were a pair of jeans I had

outgrown years before. At KISS' direction, I cut several slashes across the thighs. Squeezed into them, barely. My new red t-shirt was perfect once I cut off the sleeves and half the torso. The challenge of rock-n-roll shoes to punctuate the look solved itself as soon as I opened mother's closet. Pointed black boots with silver chains, bold zippers and a slight heel. Seamless match and I was suddenly two inches taller.

"You don't have money or a fancy car, but God gave rock 'n roll to you," Gene sang.

Is that good or bad, I wondered. I took it as good.

Heather's winked her approval.

A modern day ladies' man.

With a shake of his head, which made me suspicious, Balthazar said he would skip today's walk to school. Not like him. Did he have other plans? No time to discuss. I set out for school.

Dill met me half a block later. He didn't recognize me until we were nearly on top of one another. "Whoa! Stache, is that you?"

"I found a better way to our ladies' man," I said.

"You're wearing makeup?"

"All of us ladies' men do."

"What about Bogart and Newman and the others from yesterday?"

"Dill, those are the ladies' men of a bygone day. We are ladies' men of today. The ladies of today need a man they can relate to."

The truth was undeniable as evidenced by Dill's silence.

"I have another wig and more makeup. Let's go back to my house," I said.

"Oh, I don't know, Stache. Maybe...but I don't know..."

"Tomorrow then."

Dill peppered me with questions as we walked to school. He was most interested, strangely enough, in how tight the jeans were. "Aren't they binding and constricting in places you don't want that?" He asked several times.

As we rounded the corner to the school, I felt myself lifted off the ground. I heard a snort from behind me.

Balthazar.

He must have decided to walk to school after all.

Balthazar tossed me, not so gently, to the side.

"I can't let you do this," he said.

"Do what?"

"Imitation is only flattering to a weak man."

Riddles.

My look of bewilderment was his invitation to continue. "You are not a rock star. To imitate one in an effort to win favor with others is the act of a weak man. You are not a weak man," he explained.

"Balthazar, I am a ladies' man. This is how a ladies' man dresses," I retorted.

"No, that is how a someone who is trying too hard to be a ladies' man dresses."

"That's the point. I am trying to be a ladies' man."

"And, how did the trying work out yesterday when you threw Lindsay Jo Callahan to the ground?"

I sprang up off the grass in a rush to defend myself. Balthazar cut me short. "Don't try to tell me you were saving her," he said.

Balthazar knew me better than anyone. Every young man needed one person he could trust to point to the truth. The key was knowing when to listen and heed those words. His eyes were laser focused on me. Those giant brown orbs held me like the tractor beam in the Star Trek television show. If I am Capitan Kirk, does that make Balthazar, Spock or Bones? Can a horse go to space? Rhetorical questions for another time.

"What do I do now, Balthazar?" I said.

"The first thing you are going to do is apologize to Lindsay Jo."

He motioned behind me with his snout.

I turned to see Lindsay Jo and Bethany. I stepped onto the sidewalk. Lindsay braced herself. Still on high alert from yesterday, undoubtedly.

"Lindsay Jo, um," I cleared my throat. "I apologize for knocking you to the ground yesterday. I meant no harm and I truly hope you were not hurt."

"Stache?" She said. She must not have recognized me as I looked quite dashing. "Why are you dressed like that?" She added.

"Yeah, like I said, I am sorry Lindsay Jo."

"Strange kid."

She walked passed me.

"I'll catch up to you, Lindsay," Bethany called out. "Stache, great costume, but what are you doing? You are acting stranger than usual the last few days."

"I don't think you would understand Bethany. It's man stuff."

"Your man project? Josh told me about this. What's with the outfit?"

I remained silent, Balthazar's admonishment had me feeling self-conscious. He let out a snort. His sign for me to speak.

"I am a ladies' man," I said. There it was, I just blurted it out. Bethany didn't recoil. Surprising.

"Stache, you don't need the wig. Or the outfit," she said looking me over. "Stache, are you wearing makeup? You definitely don't need that. You are likable as you."

She rushed off to catch Lindsay.

"Sit tibi cum potestate," Balthazar said. "Be you with power."

On the walk home Balthazar explained that people who are genuine are inherently powerful. Powerful people attract others to them. "Put on's are turn off's," he said.

Heather rationalized her encouragement for the rock star outfit as a nod to her Hollywood days. "In Hollywood, we can make anyone believe anything with enough makeup," she said.

She acknowledged that the key was everyone on set was in on the lie. In the real world, that would not be the case. "Maybe," she said, "the best thing to do is be you, truthfully, and let the rest fall into place."

The list on the mirror starred back at me. I circled, Be A Ladies' Man. Next to it, I wrote, Si Fatum Habeat. If Fate Should Have It.

15

THREE HOTS AND A COT AND A PAYCHECK TO BOOT

Zeno of Citium, I believe it was, said, "Vita potest accidere per unam aestatem." A lifetime can happen over a single summer. Hollywood embraced his sentiment.

In the movie *Grease*, Danny and Sandy fell in love over the summer. This unlikely and secretive affair set the stage for a tumultuous start to their school year and some fine cinema. The movie, *Corvette Summer*, focused so intensely on the excitement of summer, that the film's makers put summer right in the title. The point being that those movies would have one believe that summers were filled with excitement and drama.

Mine seemed to come and go without life altering incidents. Returning to school each year with barely a "Nothing much. You?" In response to the all two common question, "What did you do all summer?"

The summer of my sixteenth birthday proved otherwise.

Originally, the plan for the, much needed, three-month break from school called for copious time with Dill, Tyler, and Josh. We had an elaborate array of stunts to perform and months to perfect them.

My father continued to work out of town through the school year and announced his need to continue into the summer. During the school year, his schedule hadn't mattered as I was needed at school most days. A kid loose and alone for a second summer, he felt, might not sit well with the neighbors and the social services people. A solution arose in the form of a child labor camp run by the forest service. There was a snag that nearly saved me from what I imagined were the horrors of the forest labor camp.

I was a month and a week shy of the minimum age of acceptance. This age problem vanished once the forest people found out that I would also come with my own horse. I wondered, silently, if Balthazar had been consulted. He wasn't much of the volunteer type. The forest people rationalized that since I would turn sixteen during the summer, they could overlook their own rules.

The labor camp involved 35 kids, seven adults, 42 horses, and seven mules. All of us were forced to live in the woods for two and a half months. With axes, saws, shovels, and picks, we rebuilt trails, carved new paths, and cleared underbrush. Everyone around me treated this as normal. It felt like prison to me. Even the darkest of days have shiny spots and, in this instance, those spots came in the form of cold hard cash. $3.12 per hour. Nearly, 1250 US greenbacks total.

Wealth beyond my imagination.

Balthazar fared equally well. He had negotiated a job as a supervisor over the mules so he was spared the bulk of the physical demands. Every night, as I lay my aching body down on the bare ground, he would say, "three hots and a cot and a paycheck to boot. Not a bad day, 'eh Kid?"

Balthazar could turn a stormy night into rainbow lemonade. Normally, I would've been swept up by his exuberance, but working to exhaustion each day dampened much of my enthusiasm. For him, barking orders at the mules and entertaining the other horses with stuntman tales, was pure bliss. He didn't even mind when we broke camp and moved deeper into the mountains. "The walk will do us good," he would say. He found it concerning that the other kids, and even the adults, rode their horses to the new campsite.

I was so preoccupied with survival and exhaustion I hadn't noticed the changes happening to my body.

Most boys grow. I figured that since it hadn't happened for me that it probably wouldn't. Height was an entirely biological phenomena. Genes and hormones will work their magic, or not, without much individual action to influence the outcome. The three inches of growth I experienced, though welcomed, could hardly be attributed to anything I did.

Credit only where credit is due.

The muscles on the other hand, came about through my effort. Each swing of the axe. Each shovel full of dirt. Each log hoisted. All, silently contributed to the additional twenty pounds on my growing frame.

Upon my return from labor camp, Heather could hardly contain her surprise. "Now, that's a strapping Hollywood man if I ever saw one," she said.

Three hots. A cot. A hard day's labor. A fistful of dollars. Another year older. Inches taller and stronger to boot.

I walked up to the corral the morning after our return. Balthazar would be getting hungry. "What happened to you?" He exclaimed.

"Turns out you were right about all that walking in the mountains. Does a body good," I said. He stood mouth agape. "You were too busy with your mules to notice and I was too tired to care," I added.

Self Portrait

"There's a lesson in this, Kid. For both of us," he said.

I spent the next hour and a half trying on every article of clothing in my dresser drawers and closet. Sudden human growth syndrome is accompanied by sudden shrunken clothing syndrome. An entire wardrobe is affected shoes, shirts, pants, jackets, and under things.

Long sleeves, too short. Short sleeves, too tight. Pant legs, too short. Waist bands, too tight. Shoes fit, only with toes curled.

They were all the problems I had hoped to someday have. All at once and on the night before the first day of school, however, made for an awkward moment of celebration.

The reality of the next day set in.

Heather to the rescue. "I have an idea," she said.

Visions of the lessons learned from the ladies' man experience thrust into my mind. Still, gifted horses have no flaws, right? Desperate for a solution, I took the bait.

"The clothes don't have to fit, they just have to fit in," she continued.

Riddles.

Fashion, she explained, is half choreographed and half stumbled upon. Half inspired by tailoring and half inspired by tragedy. One year, it's pants that are too big. The next, pants that are too small. Someone clips a frayed and torn shirt together with safety pins and hemp rope and, instantly, an entire social and musical genre has a uniform. Fashion trends are born from adversity and necessity.

"The key," she said, "is to wear it unapologetically. Self-consciousness and self-awareness kill the vibes."

Her pep talk, though thought-provoking, didn't help me button my pants or walk in shoes two sizes too small.

My mind drifted to Julius Caesar. I have no idea why it does such things. I had long since stopped asking "why" questions. In this case, one of Julius' phases appeared through the ether. Luicare ergo facere ius. Make a decision, then make it right.

Caesar and Heather started to make sense. I was in a narrow lane with no options but to forge forward with a bold attitude. The only wrong choice was no choice at all.

16

FASHION FOR A REVOLUTION

The entire closet and dresser were on the bedroom floor. I sifted through the pile with renewed hope. My green polo shirt with a fox sewn on the pocket was the least worst fitting. I cut off the white collar and carefully removed the pocket. In the garage, I found red, silver, and black spray paint.

Bold. Unapologetic. No thought. An artist's flow. No coloring in the lines.

The white jeans which the bully runt Stevie Fester had burned, almost to the day one year ago, provided a lush canvas.

I couldn't stop myself.

The baby blue Members Only jacket received similar treatment.

Feeling the need to go all the way, I took the only shoes that fit, tightly but fit, the scuffed and worn-through forest child labor camp issued steel-toed boots to the garage.

With the flurry of fury completed, I slept soundly knowing my fashion future had been secured. In the morning, I arranged the garments, stood back, and took in my work. The thickly painted matching ensemble of boots, pants, shirt, and jacket resembled a Jackson Pollock masterpiece.

The ill-fitting aspects of the outfit became signature fashion features. The short pant legs were tucked neatly into the calf high boots. In the pant waistband, I made four-inch vertical cuts at each hip seam. This allowed the zipper and snap button to close. I used leather straps from handles of garden tools to loosely cinch each gap in the waistband. The collarless shirt, though uncomfortably tight, was mostly hidden beneath the unzipped jacket. A roll up of the Members Only sleeves and the concealment was complete.

Style lays in the eye of the beholder.

Standing at the mirror, I was beholding the first shot fired in a fashion revolution that was hours from erupting. My schoolmates were sure to imitate, emulate, and create. Their latent talents and fashion senses simply needed a catalyst.

Fire starter. Igniter of inspiration. No longer a mere herald, a lowly Paul Revere. No, I was at the sharp end of the spear now.

Time for school.

Balthazar was unusually giddy as we started our walk to school. He mumbled something about the thrill of watching a slow motion train wreck. Dill met up with us just as I was about to ask Balthazar what he was mumbling about.

"Hey Stache, where have you been all summer?" He said. "Whoa, what happened to you?"

"Same answer to both questions, labor camp. Balthazar and I will tell you all about it on the way to school," I said.

Finally, I had something interesting to say about summer vacation. Dill hung on our every word and encouraged details about the size of the rocks and how many logs we cut and how heavy the axe was and such.

"If it means I can be as big as you, it's labor camp for me next summer," Dill exclaimed.

The reaction from the other kids at school ranged from outright disbelief to genuine interest.

Now, don't go getting the wrong image in your mind about my physical appearance. Three inches of growth got me to average for the girls. A far cry from a towering figure but a dramatic shift on me. Add to this the twenty pounds of muscle and, suddenly, school life looked promising. Like Marcus Aurelius said, "Victory is assured for he who has the momentum."

Based on the first few moments on the school's campus, victory would be mine this year.

Two years ago, I spray painted the hand-me-down ten-speed. Last year, Dill, Josh, Tyler, and I spray painted the stuntman pedal car so I knew a thing or two about spray painting. Most importantly, I knew that, while painting, the paint floats around in the garage and you can't help but breathe it into your nose. For several days, it can look like you are blowing rainbows out your nostrils. The odor of fresh paint lingers for just as long.

All this experience must have been the reason I hardly noticed the smell of my Jackson Pollock ensemble. Cutting edge revolutionary fashion has little time for the niceties of a high fluting, coifed, and perfumed society. Besides, the excitement of a new school year and a new me had my focused attention.

To be fair to myself, I do recall as I walked through the hallway that an unusual number of the kids had developed a cough over the summer. A strange occurrence, to be sure. Their contagion made me even more grateful to have spent the summer away at forest camp. My thoughts immediately went to their wellbeing. I could use some of my labor camp largess for a bushel of oranges. The fresh fruit and vitamin C would do everyone's summertime illness a bit of good. I read once that Captain Cook cured his entire crew of scurvy with just a bushel of lemons. It is hard to know what some of these kids were up to all summer so citrus as an all around cure for cold, cough, and scurvy seemed appropriate and timely.

As the morning progressed, the cough and even some light-headedness and nausea had begun to overtake my fellow class-mates. The symptoms were worsening in variety and numbers of kids inflicted. I felt the need to act as I was one of the few unaffected by the pandemic. Alas, the Principal intervened as he called me to his office during third period.

He needed a consultation. Clearly, he had not forgotten my healing talents.

"Son," he said. "you need to go home and change out of that ridiculous outfit."

I have learned that adults are last to action and first to judge. Truly original fashion never came from the mind of an adult. There was no time, however, to argue with him about style, the kids were dropping like flies. "Principal Connor, I am happy to discuss high fashion and the nuances of personal expression and functional beauty but we don't have time. The sudden outbreak of scurvy amongst the student body is more pressing. Do you happen to have oranges in the lunch room?"

"Scurvy! They are not nauseous from scurvy. They are coughing and sick from your clothes."

The revolution was inflicting casualties. I had hoped for a bloodless war. Heather was a genius. She knew that a bold expression of one's true nature, worn with unabashed confi-dence would land like a ton of bricks on the apple cart. This was my butterfly effect moment. Thoughts of the fashion hurricane hitting the runways of Milan and Paris were imprinting in my mind. Principal Conner pulled me from my imagination.

"Son, you need to go now before you inflict the whole school."

"The last thing I want is for my actions to sicken my friends, Principal Connor. I will voluntarily comply with your wishes.

Furthermore, I recognize that my avant-garde approach to my personal attire, coupled with my shocking growth, are too much. I was wrong to expect our school to absorb it all without consequence. Please accept my apologies. I will return tomorrow and, as best as I can, togged up in more muted tones," I said.

"I have no idea what you are talking about but tomorrow be in proper store clothes."

17

CLOTHES MAKE THE MAN

The forest camp cash came in handy down at Bleeker's, Timeless Fashions For a Modern World.

The Bleeker's ladies were taken by my improvised fashion and clear bend toward the exuberant. In fine company though I was, their ability to match Jackson Pollock were limited by their inventory. They pulled out the best of what they had on hand. The leather bomber jacket, hidden away in a back stock room unsold from a prior year, turned out to be the signature piece. I pushed away any article they brought that lacked a vibrant color. Once they saw the pattern develop, the ladies were in their element. They reached for clothing based on color rather than style, name brand, or gender. I didn't question their suggestions unless they reeked of tradition.

In addition to the jacket, I walked away from Bleeker's with two pair of shoes, a pair of boots, four pair of pants, six shirts, and a pack each of socks and underwear. The collection, while neither in-fashion nor out of fashion, stood out for its bright, bold, and mismatched colors. Good enough to meet Principal Connor's proper store clothes demand and expressive enough to meet my own. Though I couldn't tell you the source of my sudden style demand, I felt a need to wear my newly found confidence in my clothing. This new frame of mine required a new adornment and I was determined to provide for it.

Heather feigned a catcall when I emerged out of the bathroom the next morning. "Well, well, look out Eric Estrada, there is competition coming for you," she said.

I know I shouldn't have been, but I was addicted to her enthusiasm and unfailing endorsement. Everyone needs a cheerleader until they develop the wherewithal to be their own.

Three class periods passed without incident and I was falling into a comfort with my new self. Those positive thoughts retreated quickly as the captain of the wrestling team, Mickie Wright, approached after English class. In my experience, nothing good ever came from a wrestler headed straight for you in the hallway.

"Stache, you are looking like a stanch marsupial," he said.

Quite a compliment had he not punctuated it with a fist to my chest. I stayed silent so as to not provoke him further.

"Anyhow, Stache, the guys have been talking and we want you to join the wrestling team," Mickie continued.

The air returned back into my lungs but I was reluctant to respond for fear that I misunderstood his offer.

"Okay. Well, listen, first practice is in six weeks or so. Come try it out. You'll be a natural at it."

Again he expressed his enthusiasm with a fist to my chest.

Dill found me in the lunch room at our usual spot. "Stache, I heard you are going to join the wrestling team. I didn't know you wrestled," he said.

"Yeah, neither did I. Mickie didn't let me get a word in edgewise," I said.

"I got to thinking, Stache, we could set up a mini forest labor camp in your backyard. We could get a log to axe on. You have plenty of dirt to shovel. We will find some rocks, and maybe we could set up ropes in the trees for climbing."

"Why would you want to do that, Dill?"

Before he could respond, Bethany interrupted us.

"Hey, Stache. Hi, Dill. Congratulations on joining the wrestling team, Stache. I can't wait to watch your first match," she said.

"Uh-huh."

"Well, anyways, Jenna is wondering if you have a girlfriend or anything like that."

"To answer your question with the obvious, this is why I want to have a labor camp in your backyard. Next summer is an eternity away. I need what you got, now," Dill said.

"Well, if you two every want to eat with us, you are welcome to," Bethany said as she walked off.

The rest of our lunch was spent planning the labor camp. Dill made a drawing of my yard, complete with logs, rocks, and dirt piles noted. Something had taken hold and was driving him to a new level of enthusiasm. I couldn't help but be lifted up also.

Physical Education class was right after lunch. Mr. Riccardi, Coach, everyone called him on account of how he had been the coach of the baseball team since my dad was in school, pulled me out of the lay-up drill line.

"So, Kid," he said. "I know you are a wrestler. That's great. I think it's a good thing and I know you'll do well. But listen, fall baseball starts in six weeks and I want to see you at tryouts, alright?"

"Well, Coach...I"

He cut me off before I could start. "Don't worry. We will work it all out. Now get back in line and let me see that smooth lay-up of yours." He pushed me back toward the line.

Funny thing was, in all the years of lay-up drills in P.E. I had only made two baskets. Maybe this year would be different. Coach seemed to think so.

My last class of the day was Mr. Reston's class, American History. Lots of movies about the civil war. His was the best, he really knew what kids needed. After class he called me to his desk. "You have a sharpness about you this year, son," he said.

This day was just getting stranger and stranger.

"The student council could use a keen mind like yours. Elections are next week. I can see you as Vice-President. President maybe even. Think about it, son. It will look good on that college application," he added.

College application? I walked off in dismay.

Balthazar waited at the edge of the field behind the school. "Wrestling team, eh? That sounds like fun," he said.

"This has been an odd day, to say the least, Balthazar. Wrestling team. Sitting with the cool kids. Girlfriends. Baseball team. And, student council. Where did this come from?" I asked.

"I told you all that walking in the mountains would do you some good."

"A few inches and a few pounds. I can't imagine it makes that much of a difference."

"Yet, it has. You changed. The world reacted."

"Feels one dimensional."

Dill walked up. "The best day of your life and you are melancholy? Maybe buying me a celebratory ice cream will cheer you up," he said.

Balthazar neighed his concurrence.

I stood at the mirror that evening. No longer on the step stool. I marked a line of Le Rouge St. Germaine through Get Taller and one through Get Muscles. Vita potest accidere per unam aestatem. A lifetime can happen over a single summer.

Just like for Grease's Danny and Sandy, that school year looked to be my break-out year. And, it was only the second day.

TO THE VICTOR GOES THE CROWN

Emerging to manhood in an age of peace is a curse. Fret? Not I.

Counsel was found in the wisdom of the ancient ones. Athletic competition was their preferred method of preparation for war. It would be mine also.

"You must courageously offer your brow to the laurel wreath and your nose to the blow," said Bovier to Rousseau.

Bovier was undoubtedly reflecting on Plato, who noted that an athlete alone is too savage and a scholar to feminine. The ideal citizen is the scholar athlete. A man of thought and action. The road to discovery of the man within was paved by the the Greeks, the Sumerians, Plato and Bovier.

An athlete. A scholar. A man of action and knowledge, I shall become, I mused.

Fortunately, I wasn't alone in my man-making. Dill had found his inspiration. He plowed himself into the backyard labor camp building project. His plans, though crudely drawn, were surprisingly to scale. Within the week, we had shaped the mini labor camp.

Log chopping. Dirt shoveling. Rock lifting. And tree climbing.

Everything a young warrior-in-training needed. After school, we would rush home to the rigors of the labor camp. Dill brought an egg timer from his mom's kitchen. Set for seven minutes, we maintained our effort until the timer buzzed sending us to the next station.

The first week we could do the whole circuit only one time through. Twice through the second week.

Our strength improved.

Dill beamed at the feel of his newly forming muscles. By the end of the third week, we made it through three times in a single afternoon. We also discovered an unforeseen flaw in our design. The rocks could be lifted and moved from pile to pile and back again. Same for the dirt. The knotted rope hanging from the highest branch of the tree could be climbed over and over again.

The weak link, the log, had been axed down to chips and splinters. The Japanese maple tree from the front lawn, served us honorably but it was the only one.

Dilemma.

Solution – Mr. Wilcox.

Mr. Wilcox owned the property behind my house. Among other things, like collecting rusted cars and old tires, he brought logs from the forest to cut and sell to the townsfolk as fuel for their fireplaces and stoves. He took to watching our afterschool training and observed the demise of our log.

"Hey, Spartacus and Hercules, come here. I have a proposition for you," Mr. Wilcox called from the fence.

He had certainly overheard the chant we sang as we moved from station to station.

"Warriors forged through ancient means; blood and sweat in desert sands and gladiator rings."

Dill was quite the poet.

Credit where credit is due.

Mr. Wilcox was so inspired by our dedication and cheerful chant that he proposed a business venture. He would drop off a load of logs, Dill and I would split them into stove size pieces, reload his trailer, and Mr. Wilcox would pay us each $20.

"You two get an endless supply of warrior training and a little cash. I get chopped and stacked wood to sell. It's a win-win," he said.

Finding no fault in the arrangement we enthusiastically agreed to the terms. Week upon week passed; scholarship through the school day, warrior-ship into the afternoon.

Plato would have been proud.

Balthazar took to sitting silently with Mr. Wilcox watching our warrior training.

"Balthazar," I asked him one morning while cleaning the corral, "why haven't you said anything about our warrior training?"

"A spirit un-tested is like a dream un-lived," he said.

Riddles. I filled his water trough.

"Unless you have a determined opponent staring back at you, you will never know the limits of your man or the strength of your warrior within," he added.

Balthazar was right, of course. It was time to act. But first, I would take the matter up with Heather.

"You're procrastinating," Heather said from the bedroom before I had a chance to broach the subject.

Her voice roused me from my daydream. The man-making list stared back in the mirror. Only two items remained. Be an Athlete. Smoke Cigarettes.

"You know what you have to do," she said.

And, indeed I had known. The only way to be an athlete in the modern world was to join a team. That thought, with its notions of contrived teamwork and forced communal enthusiasms felt unnatural.

"They asked you to join the wrestling team. What more is there to think about?" She said.

"Don't forget, Kid, wrestling has an ancient and noble legacy," Walter said.

Real man stuff.

The next morning I strode confidently to Mrs. McDermott's library counter. "Mrs. McDermott, I need to see everything that the Greeks said about wrestling."

"Oh boy," she said. "Mr. McDermott loved to wrestle. He and his army buddies would get together and before you knew it, they were in the yard wrestling. They would go on for hours. He taught the kids to wrestle, including my daughters. I asked him not to, but he said that everyone needs to know how to pin a man into submission. Neither daughter is married and they are both in their 30's. A lot of good all that wrestling did them, I say."

"Mr. McDermott, once again, sounds like quite the man's man."

"Sadly, yes."

It appeared I was on my own as Mrs. McDermott fell into a state of contemplation. I found a manual on ancient wrestling and a reference book on the Sumerian, Egyptian, and Roman empires.

War. The tales of its ancient battles. Its images of muscled and hardened men clad in leather, broad sword in hand, filled my mind as I plowed through the material. Nobility and strength, valor and virtue, lifted the wars of antiquity to aspirational heights. Milo of Croton, Theagenes of Thasos, and Pythagoras of Samos, those were the idols I strived to emulate.

Body steeled through fire. Instincts sharpened through action and experience. Heart resilient through victory and defeat. If I were to be a proper man, I would also have to be war ready.

Time to talk to Dill.

"Dill," I said, my chin resting on the handle of the shovel as he lowered himself down the knotted rope, "wrestling practice starts in three weeks."

"Does that mean we have to join?"

"Well, we can't just go watch."

"Are you sure about that?"

"Dill, Balthazar has a point. If we don't test ourselves against an opponent, we will never know our strength."

"I know mine, plenty. I can climb this rope fifteen times in a single afternoon. What more do I need to know?"

"We are athletes, not sportsmen. Competition is a preparation for war."

"Stache, your fascination with ancient times makes me nervous."

"We don't have a war to prepare for, but we do have life for which to ready ourselves."

"Huh?"

"Dill..."

"I know, warriors' path, man-making stuff. I'll go. Maybe they will let us just wrestle each other."

19

NOSES OFFERED TO THE BLOW

Guided by the ancient wrestling manual, we threw ourselves into our newly chosen sport.

We added a sandpit to the labor camp training center in the backyard. According to the manual, traditional wrestling matches took place in a sandpit. We couldn't risk showing up for practice having never wrestled on the proper surface.

The next three weeks were a strict regiment of labor camp workouts, wrestling one another, and the study of ancient techniques and practices. As fortune would have it, not only was the library book filled with specific descriptions of techniques and rules, it held images of paintings on vases, panels, and tombs. Wrestling as the gods intended.

If it was good enough for the Spartans, it would be good enough for us.

Dill insisted on strict adherence to tradition.

"Now, look who is fascinated with ancient times," I told him.

We adopted the sixth century B.C. rules and practices found in the upright wrestling of the ancients.

No breaking of fingers. No strikes to the groin.

We modified the practice of athletes participating in the nude to allow an undergarment or loin cloth. We maintained the tradition of rubbing our bodies with olive oil prior to matches.

We had not wasted a single moment in those three weeks. We honed our skills and arrived at the first practice warrior ready. The mental and physical preparation of the last few months served to heighten Dill's and my enthusiasm for the battle ahead. Thinking about it, even today, I am impressed with how transformational in body and spirit that moment had been.

Dill's mother had sewn us each a custom loin cloth so as to not be embarrassed with our soiled practice cloths on our first day. A true gesture of love. She even put an extra pickle in his lunch for me. Kindness impossible to repay.

Dill and I walked into a locker room full of our fellow wrestling aspirants.

"Stache. Dill. Glad you guys made it," team Captain, Mickie Wright, said as he approached from around a bank of lockers. "You are just in time. Coach is about to start practice."

"Okay, men," Emphasis on men. I knew we were in the right place. "strip down to your tighty whites. First up. We are going to weigh each of you. I want to know how we look for the weight classes. I don't want any forfeits this year."

He blew his whistle. Forty kids were nearly naked in an instant. I stood, immobile, but in awe. I saw that Dill hadn't moved either.

That is a magical whistle, I thought.

"You two," coach pointed to Dill and me. "Did you not hear the whistle?"

"Yes," Dill said.

He was holding his own pretty well.

"Your first time out for the team, right?" coach said.

Obviously, he recognized our advanced skill, even though the school clothes hid our physiques.

Wrestler knows wrestler.

"If you move slow in wrestling, you lose the match. You move slow in life, you fall behind. Isn't that right, men?" coach yelled.

The team members responded with a scream of, "Yes, coach." The voices of the new kids, working hard to keep up with the ritualistic culture, trailed the collective response by a fraction of a second. This created an echoed sound through the locker room.

"You two are already falling behind. Now, get undressed. We are going to do some warm up exercises after the weigh in. That will be your chance to catch up, got that?"

The kids all fell into a silent line that started in the hallway outside the coach's office and ran back into the locker room. Dill and I found our spot at the end of the line.

As we neared the coach's office, the situation became clearer. An assistant coach would take our name, age, grade, and home-room teacher's name. We would enter the coach's office, stand on the scale, the assistant coach would yell our weight, and we walk out. Simple as that.

Having been the last two kids to weigh in, we joined the rest of the team in the locker room. The coach entered shortly their after.

"Okay. I need to talk to," he looked at his clip board. "Tommy, Dill, and Stache. Are these their real names?" He asked the assistant who nodded and shrugged his shoulders. "The rest of you are going to get suited up and meet Coach J in the gym. Move it." He blew his whistle and the chaos ensued. Coach motioned to the three of us to follow him down the hall.

Dill and I knew Tommy. Two Finger Tommy, they called him. He was a funny sort. Always laughing and making others laugh also. He didn't care too much for the school stuff but he liked being at school and talking with the other kids. Kind of the opposite of Dill. Despite the differences, those two got along and Dill would help Tommy with his homework at times.

They called him Two Finger Tommy on account of how he only had two fingers on his left hand. His dad owned the same lumber yard that Fin worked at when he died. When Tommy was eight, he was helping his dad. As Tommy says it, he took his eye off the blade. "My dad said I was lucky I didn't lose the whole arm." He would say to anyone who asked.

Since then Tommy, out grew most everyone at the school.

"Fellows," the coach started, "I have some disappointing news. Tommy, the maximum weight allowed by the state's rules is 285 pounds. You are at 332 pounds. I don't see you loosing the weight you have to and putting it back on in the form of muscle in time for any of our meets. You two, Dill and Stache, you have the opposite problem. 106 pounds is the lightest class. You two are at 99 and 103 pounds. Not horrible and you would still be able to wrestle but I already have four kids with experience on the team wrestling for only two slots in that class. I don't see how you are going to be able to compete. Sorry boys. I suggest you do some work through the off season and try again next year."

With that he grabbed his clipboard, escorted us to the locker room, and rejoined the practice with a blow into his whistle.

"What are we going to do now, Stache?" Dill asked.

"We torch on to Olympia, Dill."

20

SPARTANS VERSE SAMURAI

When Dill got on a track nothing would take him off.

"Let's talk about Olympia over a cone at Custard's Last Stand," Dill said.

"Great idea. Tommy, you want to come with us?" I asked.

"Naw, I better get to the yard. My dad has a big order to get out today. He'll need some help."

"Are you doing okay, Tommy?" Dill asked.

"Oh yeah. This was my mom's idea. My dad will be happy. More time for cutting lumber. I'll see you guys tomorrow."

Josh and Tyler were seated outside making short work of their cones as we got to Custard's. "How was wrestling practice?" Tyler said.

"Plato wouldn't have recognized it," I said.

The conversation quickly settled onto more casual topics but my mind was churning on what to do next.

"Track team practice starts in a few months," I said to Dill on the way home.

"I am done joining, Stache. If I am warrior trained I am

going to be warrior tested also. That is what you promised, isn't it?"

Dill had a point. Do the work, reap the reward.

We were halfway down Main Street when we heard Balthazar neigh. There he was at the far end of the alley that sat between Dirty Dick's and Bleeker's. Clearly, he wanted our attention.

"Hey Balthazar, what are you doing down here?" I asked as we approached him.

He gave a snort and a nod to the doorway in front of which he was standing. The sign read, Takahashi's Combat Arts Authentic Karate. New Student Special.

Like they say, when the student is ready, the mana will fall from the heavens.

Dill and I stepped through the strings of cloth hanging in the doorway. We were instantly transported to the land and time of another ancient warrior culture.

Several men stood in a squatted stance in front of a board wrapped in canvas and affixed to the floor. They were striking it with their fists over and over. Two others were faced off. One grasped the other and threw him over his shoulder landing him hard on the floor. At the center of the red painted floor was a single man, standing perfectly still, sword in hand, dressed in a strange robe. His sword suddenly thrust forward. His body pulled by the sword. The man's sword moved up and down, forward and back. It circled left to right thrusting forward at each change of direction. The movements, the sword, were mesmerizing. Sword and man were one. Each came to a complete stop just as suddenly as they had started.

He approached us. "You must be Dill and Stache, yes?" He asked.

Mr. Takahashi, Sensei Takahashi, we learned had moved from Japan to the United States to be near his daughter who was studying to be a doctor in the major city ninety-seven miles away. After a year in the city, he wanted a small town life like he was accustomed to in Japan. Sensei was a descendent of samurai warriors. His family had practiced the same form of sword and hand-to-hand combat since the 14th century.

Samurai warriors. Tradition. Discipline. Hard work.

Dill and I had found our home.

The training was rigorous. Horse stance pose for fifteen minutes. Punching a makiwara board until our knuckles bruised. Marching across the floor of the dojo kicking for hours. Front kicks. Side kicks. Roundhouse kicks. Spinning kicks. Flying kicks. Throws. Joint locks. Strikes. If we weren't with Sensei, we were practicing in the sand pit at the backyard labor camp.

Sensei had only two rules for sparring, no padding and wear a mouthguard. The mouthguard was to keep our teeth from cutting the other's fist.

Real warrior training. Real warrior forging. Real warrior testing.

Every few weeks, Sensei would scream "kumite". Spar. We would attack him with everything we had. The harder we fought the easier it was for him to defeat us.

"Sensei, why can't we land even one strike against you?" Dill asked after one such session.

"You fight, you attack, to land a punch or kick. I defend, I attack, to end the fight, to end your life. This is the warrior's way to fight. Your fighting is a sport. My fighting is my life."

"Sensei, I don't want to end Dill's life or yours," I said.

"Yes. I don't want to hurt you and I don't want to be hurt. This is the paradox of training to be warrior. We train killing skills to preserve life. We need one another to practice for a real fight. The intensity must be high to challenge my skill but not so high that I don't survive. Train harder. Become stronger. Move faster. Do this together and you will arrive at the threshold separating training and combat. Separating sportsman and warrior. Separating boy and man."

We were hooked.

Run around a track. Throw a ball. Wrestle with rules. None could match Sensei Takahashi's call to the boy to become a man.

"Balthazar," I said to him as I filled his water trough one morning, "how did you know to show us Mr. Takahashi's dojo?"

"He found me. I was walking through town on the very day he arrived. He called to me with an offer to share his apple. We talked. He asked where I lived and who it was I lived with. I told him all about you and Dill. In particular, your man-making journey. On your first day of wrestling practice, I went to see him to tell him that you were taking one more step toward manhood. He asked me to wait for you in the alley by the door."

"How could he know we wouldn't stay at wrestling?"

"Hana yori dango, he said. Dumplings over flowers. He guessed, based on your labor camp training, that you would prefer substance over appearances and conversely, the team would prefer appearances over substance."

I stood at the mirror no longer feeling that Le Rouge St. Germaine looked good on me. Heather had remained quiet throughout our wrestling and samurai training.

"Why haven't you crossed through Be an Athlete?" She called from the other room.

"How can I. The wrestling team did not want me and I can't bring myself to join any other team?"

"Walter and I play a team sport. But the lesson is not in joining a team or even playing sports. It is about pushing yourself mentally, spiritually, and physically. It is about knowing yourself. Neither jersey nor trophy matter."

A Le Rouge St. Germaine line through Be an Athlete.

I knew myself. Did others know me, I wondered.

Some say that a soaring bird unseen has never flown.

Who was I, but that lowly bird with its amazing gift of flight, unseen, simply unknown. A man unflaunted (I know, but it should be a word) remains invisible.

Unknowable. Unseeable.

21

SMOKE SCREENS, SECRETS, AND SHAMANS

My reflection in the mirror. The man emerging, I knew him. I saw him. Soon, the world would also.

The final man-making action item would be my soaring act for all to see. Like the greats, Bogart, Dietrich, Eastwood, Doc Holliday, Churchill, and Popeye the Sailor Man, smoking, cigarettes, cigars, or pipes, would be my signature. My synonym. My definition.

I wiped the Le Rouge St. Germaine from my lips. Yes, self-adornment was once again pleasurable. It helped that I had seen photos of Samurai dressed in Kabuki makeup in Sensei's family photo album.

Manly is as manly does.

Time to find cigarettes. Time to find Dill.

"I don't know, Stache. Is smoking really the only way?" Dill said on the walk to school.

"It's the final step, Dill."

"Well the other steps don't seem to be making a difference. Maybe I am happy just being, even if that means that others don't see me as a man. I still think I am."

"It is not about how you feel, it is about how others see you.

With a cigarette hanging from your lips, they won't be able to deny your manhood anymore."

"If I am going to be a man who smokes then my cigarettes are going to say something about me."

"The cigarette doesn't matter. It's the act that matters."

"Really, Stache? After all we have been through? Let me point out that we didn't just wrestle. We wrestled the way the gods intended. The way Plato and the Spartans did. When that didn't work out, Mr. Takahashi showed us the ancient way of the Samurai. We turned our backyard labor camp into a business venture. We didn't just get dirty, we learned real stuntman skills and tested our resolve. We are not the kind of men who shove any old fire stick in our mouths."

"That's good, Dill. That's real good. You should write that down. And you are correct. But I don't know anything about cigarettes."

"Time to learn up then, isn't it?"

I left Dill at Corridor A and headed to the library.

"Mrs. McDermott," I said approaching her perch.

"You again. I heard the wrestling didn't work out so well."

"All for the best. I am here on another matter."

"The suspense is unbearable."

"I'll need to see your section on smoking."

"Well, now you are finally onto a proper topic."

"Really?"

"Indeed, Mr. McDermott and I still enjoy sharing a cigarette after ..." She stopped mid sentence. Her complexion turned a rosy red. "...em, well...after dinner, now and again. Let me show you the material we have."

On the shelf were a dozen books on the health effects of smoking and the cigarette manufacturing industry.

I already knew my growth would be stunted and my lungs

would turn black and any child I carried in my womb would have six toes. That was sixth grade health class stuff.

"Mrs. McDermott, I know I shouldn't smoke. If, suppose for a minute I wanted to, how do I decide which cigarette to smoke? Do you have a book on that?"

"Before you can answer that question you should understand why you would want to smoke?"

"To be, no to show others that I am a man."

"Sounds like you need to go back a little further in time to understand the meaning of smoking."

She walked. I followed.

She pulled a book from the shelf. *Shamanistic practices of the indigenous peoples of the Americas*. "Yes. Here we go. Chapter ten, ceremonial use of tobacco, related plants and herbs."

Over the next hour, I learned; tobacco had an ancient history of use to bring boys from adolescence to manhood; was used for specific healing and ritual; and the tobacco of the ancients is not the tobacco of the Marlboro Man.

"Dill," I found him sitting at our lunch spot. "I have good news and bad news."

"Good news first."

"It doesn't matter what brand of cigarettes. The whole thing is a lie."

"And the bad news."

"We need to find a shaman. A tribal shaman."

"A what?"

I filled him in on the details of my research over a butter and jelly sandwich. Dill had egg salad.

"Do we know any shamans?" I asked.

"They must be everywhere. Have you seen how many men are running around doing man things?"

"You are right. Simply a matter of asking around."

Which is exactly what we did. We asked every man we knew;

Principal Conner, Mr. Jasper, the manager at Custard's Last Stand, Mr. Grady, the school's custodian, Coach Riccardi, the P.E. teacher, and Mr. Reston, the history teacher. The response from each was the same. "I have no idea what you're talking about." Or some variation, thereof.

I even asked Dodge Nickels, quarterback for the football team. He laughed and walked off.

Surely all these men couldn't have become men without a medicine man and a ceremony to welcome them to manhood. Native American Tribal lands abutted our town in all directions, after all!

After school, Dill and I were in the backyard labor camp.

"Mr. Wilcox," I said, as he came to the fence. "will you introduce us to your shaman?"

"Well now, that is an interesting question. Why do you two need a shaman?"

Promising. He knew something but was going to make us work for it. Man tactic. That was a game I was well-practiced at.

"We have to complete one more task to becoming a man," I said.

"Is that so?"

"Yes. We have to smoke cigarettes but it turns out that without a shaman, smoking has no man result. Though, I suspect you already know this."

"You boys have been working real hard the last few months. Working for me. Working for yourselves, here, in your labor camp. Working with Mr. Takahashi. Working at school. The question to ask yourselves is why is that not enough?"

"Exactly," Dill said. "with all that we are doing, why does no one see us as men?"

He looked contemplatively toward the sky. He reached into his shirt pocket, withdrew a cigarette, placed it gently in his mouth and lit it. Classic manliness. It was a sight to behold.

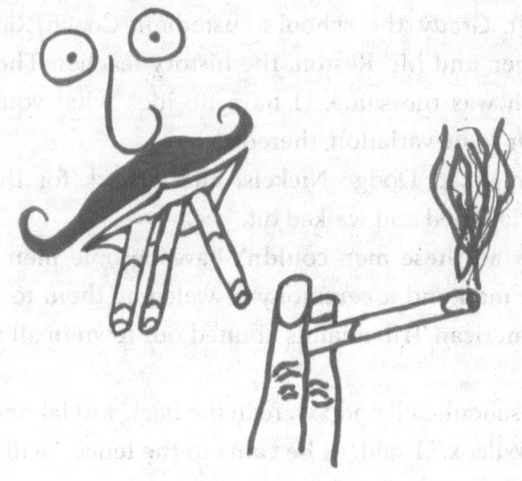

He exhaled a long stream of smoke.

"People only see what they want to see. If you wait around for the world to tell you who you are, you'll be waiting a long time and you won't like the answer," Mr. Wilcox said. "See you boys tomorrow."

He walked off.

"What are we going to do now, Stache?" Dill said.

"Did you see how he smoked that cigarette. Glorious. We need to be smokers."

22

COWBOY KILLERS

"Stache!"

"I know. We need a shaman," I said. Dill was a task master.

The next morning, I found myself back in the library.

"Mrs. McDermott, how did Mr. McDermott become a man? Did he have a shaman?"

"I don't know. He left to the Army, then to the war, a boy. He returned a man. What happened in between he doesn't talk about."

Silence. Secrets. Man code stuff.

That night, Heather held firm to her list. "If you are not seen as a man, there is no value. The whole point of the list is to show everyone you are a man."

"There must be more to this man stuff. The shaman ceremony feels like it has real meaning."

"The shaman's world is not yours. It is only meaningful if it has relevance in your world. Smoking cigarettes and all the other items on the man-making list have meaning in your world."

I thought this last act would be the easiest thing on the list.

Get a cigarette. Smoke a cigarette. Man-making. How did this get so complicated, I wondered.

Dill was waiting for me at the end of the drive in the morning.

"Dill, good news and bad news," I said.

"Bad news first," he said.

"The shaman's magic won't work on us."

"And, the good news?"

"We get to smoke cigarettes." I explained Heather's rational.

"Since we have no alternatives, I want to smoke the cowboy killers. Marlboro Reds. Mr. Wilcox smokes them and I like Mr. Wilcox."

"That works for me. We can stop by the store on the way to school."

Balthazar snorted. His tone was troubling. No time to discuss. We stepped into the Clyde's Grocery and Sundries.

"We will need two packs of Marlboro Reds," Dill announced to the store's clerk.

"You have to be eighteen years old to buy tobacco. Are you eighteen?" she asked.

"Eighteen?"

Dill was doing great.

"When did that rule happen?" I added.

"Well, by the late 1890's most states had age restrictions on the sale of tobacco. Those ranged from fourteen to nineteen years old. Or in some cases an outright ban on the sale. The modern regulatory system of a federal minimum age restriction dates to 1968. Not that any of this matters to your situation. Clearly, you are too young, at nearly any point in the history of the sale of cigarettes, to buy cigarettes."

Balthazar gave a slight chuckle as we emerged from Clyde's.

When we got to school, I went straight to the back of the Industrial Arts Building. That was where the bad kids hung out, smoking and drawing skulls on the side of the building. Carlos Constanza was their ring leader. They called him Charlie the Chimney on account of how much he smoked.

"Hey Charlie," I said in the most casual of voices.

"Hey Stache. What are you doing back here?"

"I need to get some cigarettes. Clyde's wouldn't sell me any. I figured you would know where I could buy a couple of packs."

"They will stunt your growth." The whole gang of kids erupted in laughter.

"Yeah. Might."

"Oh, I am just messing with you, Stache. You're alright and Balthazar is aces. Listen, my dad buys me all the cigarettes I want. The only catch is I have to pay him."

"He does?"

"He started smoking when he was ten. Hasn't stopped yet and he is in great shape. He says the government is full of it with all its warnings and restrictions. He says if the government is involved then freedom pays the price. Buying me cigarettes is his way of keeping America free, he says."

"Sounds like quite a man's man."

"Might be. So, the thing is he charges me a little extra for doing it. I do the same for anyone who wants a pack."

"Not sure I have options. Do you have two packs you can sell me?"

"Come by my locker after school. Ten bucks a pack."

"Thanks, Charlie."

He was good to his word. Two packs of Camel Lights. Joe Camel, complete with sunglasses, on the wrapper. Dill and I went to Custard's to celebrate the first day of the rest of our lives.

Josh and Tyler arrived just as we sat down.

"Hey Stache. Hey Dill," Tyler said.

"My sister said you guys are going to smoke cigarettes. Can we watch?" Josh said.

We hadn't even smoked a single cigarette. We were already known as men who smoked. Magic. Heather was right.

"Sure," Dill said.

After Custard's we sat in my backyard. With the package of matches I grabbed from the drawer next to the stove, we mimicked Mr. Wilcox's style.

Time to light up.

Dill lit a match, pushed both cigarette and match to his face. He gave the Camel a gentle inhale. It refused to light.

"No Dill. Let me show you." My confidence was bolstered by the knowledge that the kids at school already knew us as smokers. Cigarette in mouth, lit match in hand, I drew in a lung full of air through the Camel Light filter with the strength of a deep sea diver.

The body can forget things when the mind is focused. I am still confused as to how it happened. The lips, tongue, and teeth failed to coordinate with the diaphragm. Had everyone worked together, the cigarette would not have been swept with the air to the back of my throat. I also would not have burnt my lip and palette. Nor would I have vomited while gasping for air.

Dill, ever the stickler for safety and emergency response, quickly grabbed the garden hose and doused, what he surely thought to be a fire in my mouth, with several gallons of water. More coughing. More choking.

"Work to maintain a beginner's mind," Sensei Takahashi always said.

In that spirit, I attributed our less than successful first attempt to lack of practice.

Dill and I were tenacious, if nothing else.

We made the appropriate adjustments to our technique.

Dill relit his first cigarette.

23

FINAL ACT - MAN MADE

By the fifth cigarette, we had the cough-less inhale and exhale down pad. The sixth and seventh cigarette we worked on our style. Dill emulated Mr. Wilcox. Slow draw in. Smooth long exhale. Smoke lingering.

I chose the classic James Dean lean against the tree, one foot up on the trunk, cigarette hanging off a half open bottom lip. Not so much consuming the cigarette as wearing it. Josh and Tyler were impressed.

The eighth cigarette, half smoked, the serpentine ash dangled from the end awaited a flick. I didn't get the chance. The dizziness came on fast and strong. I woke with my face in the dirt. Dill was on all fours trying to catch his breath. Tyler and Josh were standing at the ready, garden hose in hands.

The sudden reoccurrence of unexplained fainting concerned me. More immediately, however, was the lack of warning on the cigarette package. I made a note to research the warning label requirements. Clearly, two of us vomiting from the cigarettes was more than coincidence.

How long had the cigarette company people known about this, I wondered.

The next morning, I went to see The Chimney.

"Charlie, your dad is selling cigarettes without proper warning labels," I said as I thrusted the half smoked packs of Camel Lights into his abdomen. "I imagine in the illicit cigarette trade refunds are not customary. I expect consideration of a partial refund non-the-less. Defects are defects."

"Stache, what are you talking about?" Charlie said.

"The fainting. The fainting is what I am talking about." I turned on my heels and left. No need to belabor the point. Charlie knew what he had to do to make things right.

Dill and I were enjoying our lunch when Charlie approached.

"You are lucky there is a market for individual cigarettes. I have a restocking fee but I am willing to buy back your cigarettes. $0.50 each. Six bucks per pack."

He tossed twelve dollars on the table and walked away. It was the first and only time anyone remembered seeing Charlie in the lunch room.

"Well, how about that?" Dill said.

"You know, Dill, he..." I was interrupted by Bethany's sudden appearance

"Stache. Hey Dill. Stache, look you don't have to smoke cigarettes to be cool."

"Em..."

"Josh told me what happened yesterday. Charlie isn't cool because he smokes. He is cool because he can draw. And not just the skulls on the back of the shop building. He drew my portrait. It was very sweet."

"I don't draw, Bethany."

"That's not the point Stache. Other things make you, you. Maybe you don't show them all the time, but they are there."

"They are?"

"Well, don't start smoking. Besides, it will stunt your growth."

Balthazar was quiet on the walk home. At the corral, I broached the subject.

"Balthazar, why are the man-making things dangerous?" I said.

"Are they?"

"Yes. Smoking causes vomiting, shortness, and black lung. Getting in fights causes black eyes and broken noses. Being a ladies' man causes stomach aches and hyperventilation. Stunt-manning causes ruptured spleens. Mustaches cause fainting spells. Bravery causes bleeding of the head."

"You've been thinking about this."

"Even getting muscles came with a price. What good has any of it done, anyway?"

"Responsum est in morte. The answer lies in death," he said.

Riddles.

"You think there is a magic moment at which the man suddenly appears," he continued.

"Doesn't he?"

He laughed. "A weak man is focused solely on the result. A strong man knows that the result, the true impact to self, has no relation to the outcome of a single act."

"Why does the answer lie in death?"

"There is no room for the man as long as the child exists."

"I feel like I have come close to not existing several times. Does that count?"

"Depends on what meaning you choose to give to those moments."

More riddles.

"You have the power to decide. If the list," he continued. "incites a belief that you are a man, then it works. If, on the other hand, you only see failure, then you will always be a child."

That night, the list in the mirror looked back at me.

I didn't like smoking cigarettes and I didn't want to be a chimney like Charlie.

I was an athlete. I felt strong and capable in Sensei's dojo. A competition for the sake of proving my worth, was unattractive to me. Besides, the race was against myself and I showed up at the starting line everyday.

My ability to use my body means more than what its lengths and weights are. Weights and measures make not the man.

Ladies' man, not ladies' man. I get to choose the meaning of this. If that is true, then I could choose the timing also.

I allow myself to be who I am without fear. Along the way I might get dirty but I relentlessly march on.

With Sensei's training, I move through life as a warrior, arriving in peace but always prepared to fight.

I might never be able to grow a mustache but that will not prevent me from being a man. Like smoking, a real man doesn't allow externalities to define him.

My man-making was not left to fate. Deterministic effort undefined by others. Brave and courageous through action. Through adversity. Earned.

I was a man. I could see him staring back at me. I knew him. I admired him. Like a peacock, it was time for him to fly.

I struck a line of Le Rouge St. Germaine through Smoke Cigarettes.

24

WHEN NO OTHER NAME WILL DO

Turns out I was wrong. Man-making is about public performance. All day. Everyday. In every way. Exhausting. This dose of reality came in swift and heavy. Like acne on picture day. The family motto had nearly vanished from my mind. I should have maintained the vigilance. A bad day can always get worse.

Parades and pageants. Not sure either has a place outside of the military and pets. They certainly have no place in high school. Especially, the pageants. My views were hardened from personal experience.

Each year, the state's annual Ms. Teen Pageant (its a real thing) needed contestants. The pageant people figured a high school would be a good place to find girl teens to participate. Normally, sound logic. The prior three years, had shown the flaw in their methodology.

My first period teacher, Mrs. Belsky, had a stack of envelopes at the corner of her desk. My mind drifted as a young man's often does at 7:45am.

"The Ms. Teen Pageant applications have arrived. When I

call your name, please come up and get your packet. Good luck, girls," she said.

She pulled the first envelope, "Jenna Parker."

The memories rushed in. Along with the dread. All my man-making work was about to disappear into an ash heap. Despite my best efforts to counteract the Ms. Teen Pageant forces, they had continued to include me, well, my name, on the invitees list. I couldn't blame them. Mine was a girl's name.

One by one, the girls rose at the call of their names.

I held my breath. Hope beyond hope that this year they received my note, *My name and gender don't match. Inconvenient, I know. Please remove me from your list. I am a teen boy not a teen girl.* Written on the envelope next to *Return to Sender.* Maybe that three-times-is-a-charm thing worked.

"Oh my," Mrs. Belsky said. She read the final name.

My name. Out loud for all to hear. A pageant packet? Again.

Silence. Thank goodness. Nobody heard.

Thunderous laughter erupted. Several of the boys fell out of their desks, doubled over on the floor. Uncontrollable. They heard.

Mrs. Belsky's half-hearted attempt at order was hampered by her own stifled giggles. She waved the packet, my packet, high above her head. The outburst unmuted. She stood. Classroom order returned. She took the opportunity to personally deliver the Ms. Teen Pageant packet to my desk.

I didn't move. Frozen in a reluctant acceptance of my fate. The world would never know me as a man. I had a girl's name. A woman's name. And that was that.

The rest of the school day did nothing to diminish my fatalistic thoughts. The boys asked me if I had picked out a bikini and dress to wear for the competition. The girls just giggled as I walked through the halls. The entire school knew. They laughed therapeutically.

I did not.

Custard's Last Stand, my sanctuary. The ice cream cone helped change the mood. Dill kept the conversation light. We made plans for the summer and our next backyard adventures. Josh and Tyler soon joined in the celebration.

My man had suffered a setback.

"Shake it off, Kid," Balthazar said that night. "Externalities don't make the man."

"Logic's end is despair, Balthazar. Isn't that your saying?" I said. "This Pandora can't be put back in a box. For the rest of my life, whether I am introduced in person or through correspondence, it will be with this name. A first impression impossible to overcome."

"Well, if the name is the problem, change it."

Hope. Tunnel light. Logic without despair.

"I can do that?"

Heather agreed, "We change our names all the time in Hollywood."

New life pumped into my man corpse.

New challenge, too. What to name oneself? No small decision. A new name to make a statement about who I am. Who I am not. To overcome the physical disadvantages. That was a tall order for a name and one I didn't take lightly. Sleep brought commitment to the plan but no answer to the name question.

"Dill," I announced with confidence. "I am going to change my name."

"Why? I like Stache."

"No. My real name."

"Right. Yeah, probably for the best. What are you going to name yourself?"

"I don't know yet."

"Hey how about, Mack Macho or Rico Suave that will be a good one. Ooh, Luther Lionheart, no, Mitch Manly."

"Dill, I am not sure about those."

"Well, if you are going to do it, figured you better go in the opposite direction of your given name."

"True."

We enlisted Sensei Takahashi's help after school.

"I have known ten Sota's. All of them are very big men. Sota means violent wind. Sota-son. Oh, how about Akio. It means manly hero. Akio-son. I like them both. Now, more push ups then hit the makiwara board for ten minutes."

We were off to a good start.

Mr. Wilcox, suggested that it might be impractical to take the name Butch Cassidy. "People might think you are trying to steal the first Butch Cassidy's image and appeal."

"That's exactly what I am doing. I thought that was the whole point of Balthazar's plan."

"In principle, yes. The point isn't to take another man's manliness, but to find your own."

Everyone seemed to have a habit of speaking in riddles when teaching life lessons.

"How about Elliott Ness or James Bond?" I said. "They roll off the tongue and exude man-ness."

"You missed the point. Those men earned their manliness and now you have to earn yours. I recognize the handicap of your current name but there are no shortcuts in life, son," he said.

"How about Umberto? It has a hairy-chested sexiness to it," Dill said.

If it were simple, everyone would do it, I thought.

"I have been thinking. How about Ramesses, Tiberius, or Khan," Balthazar suggested through his evening oats and apple snack.

Only one day and I already had quite a list of potential

names gathered. More research would be needed. I went straight to the library the next morning.

25

THE FIRST DAY OF THE REST OF YOUR LIFE

"Oh good. I was hoping to see you today," Mrs. McDermott said as I approached. "I heard what happened yesterday with the pageant business. I mentioned it to Mr. McDermott. He sent me with this book for you." She pushed, *The passage: ten tales every young Scot needs to read* across the counter.

"I am not Scottish."

"Well, Mr. McDermott is and he said the stories helped him when he was your age."

I retreated to a quiet corner of the library and read the first story.

Ronan, the young hero, was sent on an errand through his home valley and over a mountain to the adjacent valley. His journey, as journeys are want to, goes awry as Ronan gets lost. Dangers lurk in quiet places, as we all know, and Ronan's journey was through just such a quiet place.

Ronan was carrying his dead father's dirk which his living uncle thrust into his hands just as he left the village. You can guess the rest.

Trolls and beasts. Brandishing of the dirk. Courage to kill. Courage to befriend the friendless, and such.

The dirk, however, caught my imagination. I learned through the description in the tale that a dirk is a short-bladed sword or a long-bladed knife with a substantial handle. A dirk's design made it most effective in forward thrusting movements, should one find oneself in a mano-a-mano battle with man or beast.

Ronan's dirk had a legend and magical power attached to it. Both led him to unknown truths about his father and Ronan's personal destiny.

Gold in the very first story.

"Please extend my deepest gratitude to Mr. McDermott. The book has been as important to me as it was to him," I said as I pushed it across the counter toward Mrs. McDermott.

I found Dill.

"Dill, I have it. My name is Dirk," I said.

"Dirk. Rakish. Brash. Manly. I like it."

Balthazar was equally impressed. "And, what about your last name?"

"I already have a last name."

"It won't do. Your parents have been all but absent from your journey. A final symbolic act. If you are going to become your own man, a new last name is necessary."

Balthazar, brilliant as always, knew his stuff.

Dirk Necessary.

Time to go to the court.

"Name changes on the third Thursday of the month," the court clerk said.

Only one week to wait. Stars aligned.

There were four name changers in the courtroom that day. The first, a divorcee who wanted her maiden name back. The second was the town hippie who had run for mayor twice. "Third time is a charm." He told the judge. He was changing his name to Mayor Lord Over Us. "So, residents would call to me on the streets, Mayor Mayor Lord Over Us."

I was third up. "I am changing my name to protect the inno-cent," I said. I feigned a suspicious tone for a little intrigue. I stole the line from the introduction to a television show that was on every afternoon on the UHF station. You probably remember it. "The names have been changed to protect the innocent." The announcer stated at the beginning of each show.

"Why do the innocents need protecting?" Asked the judge.

"With such a dynamic and clearly masculine name as Dirk Necessary, my parents, the town, and, dare I say, the state should not be held responsible for the awe that will accompany my thrusting forward," I said.

The judge was rendered speechless in his recognition of the truth.

"Son, are your parents here to sign for you?"

"Parents?"

"I am signing for him, Your Honor," a voice said from the back of the court room. Mr. Wilcox's voice.

"Fine. Next?" The judge said.

The final name changer was a girl. One year older than me. She was changing her name to Feral Medusa d'Vie. She wore a bright cyan suit with a red tie. She had pinned and clipped her hair tight to her scalp with dozens of bobby pins and hair fasteners. It gave the impression that she was holding back all the snakes of Medusa legend. The Judge asked her reason for the name change.

"To roar," she said. "to live and love with a passion of a thousand wild beasts. To live the life that Darla Ann Holmes simply could not."

"Oh boy," the judge said.

Captivating. I was enthralled and needed to know her. The thought of which made my stomach flip. Vulnerability and fear, my familiar friends returned. Would they ever not be here, I wondered.

The judge's voice filled the courtroom and pulled me back to the light.

"Carol Miller, Mayor Lord Over Us, Dirk Necessary, Feral

Medusa d'Vie, please rise, raise your right hand, and repeat after me."

Dirk Necessary. Spoken for all to hear. I looked out to the street at Balthazar who was standing below the open window listening to the proceedings. With a short snort, he straightened up a little taller. I was sure I saw a tear roll from his cheek.

Dirk Necessary isn't shy. Dirk Necessary isn't afraid to talk to Feral Medusa. That much I was sure of.

The hearing ended. I walked directly to Feral and said, "Hello Feral Medusa d'Vie, I am Dirk Necessary."

"And so you are, Dirk Necessary," she said. "Call me Maddie, Maddie d'Vie." We took a few steps towards the door. She continued, "You know, I've seen you walking around. You and your horse. Always talking, you two. Real serious like, it seems."

"Balthazar? Who better to talk to than family, right?" I said. She smiled a question but thankfully didn't ask. "You two will get along like butterscotch ripple and vanilla. Speaking of which, how do you feel about ice cream cones, Maddie d'Vie?"

Dill rushed us before she had a chance to answer. "She loves them and so do I. Mr. Wilcox said it's his treat today." He reached his hand toward Maddie. "Ms. d'Vie, pleasure to meet you. My name is Dill."

"Pleasure is all mine, Dill."

"And you sir," Dill turned toward me. Stood a little taller, squared his shoulders, and offered his hand with authority. "Mr. Dirk Necessary, welcome to the first day of the rest of your life."

The End

ABOUT THE AUTHOR

Kelly S. Ward is a man. Resist the urge to ask if he is Irish. He is not. Parental naiveté is the only good explanation for the name. A lifetime of impact, through an assumption that the world is not this cruel.

Unsurprisingly, he writes about masculinity, believing that the overly simplistic labels of masculine and feminine fail as an explanation for our beautifully complex beings. Life under this dualistic regime denies us the opportunity to live fully within ourselves.

He writes about the outliers. Those who call to us to resist the social demands that herd us into a narrow existence. Though scorned and rejected, these truth seers illuminate and enrich our lives. We are all outliers. It's the universe's gift most of us never unwrap.

As a recovered political campaigner and government cog, he writes about the unseen and unnamed forces that shape our world. For him, *The Matrix* and *Parks and Rec* are documentaries. A tough reality for his idealistic mind to accept. However, admitting the problem was his first step to recovery.

Dirk Necessary: A Man's Man Journey, is his first novel.

 instagram.com/kellys.ward

9 798993 087511